SNADER
PUBLISHING CO.

About the Book

Eden didn't peg bribery, kidnapping, and murder for summer activities.

For eighteen-year-old Eden, her court-mandated community service is set to be every bit as punishing as prison. Sent off to work at a pizza joint while living with her grandmother in a little out-of-the-way town, at least she can appreciate the peace and quiet.

But the town is hiding its own secrets, and pretty soon peace and quiet will be very hard to come by. She might not realize it, but between the spiteful neighbor, the enigmatic mayor, and the calculating owner of the abandoned hospital, Eden's ninety days in Halstead are set to be the most exciting of her life.

Follow Eden's unexpected adventure in this strange and entertaining tale of mystery.

When the Time is Right is the start of the Halstead Mystery Series.

About the Author

Bill Bush grew up a Wildcat, graduating from Yates Center High School in 1985. The only other place he has lived for more than ten years is in Halstead, where he's been since 2008.

His dream is to become a full-time fiction author. He took a step in that direction in 2018 by joining Kansas Publishing Venture as a newspaper reporter. Now he writes nonfiction during the day and fiction at night.

Besides the Halstead Mystery series, Bill is the author of the Vetrix series, has published a book of poetry, several collections of short stories, and a compilation of his newspaper columns that have appeared in the Harvey County Independent since April, 2013.

Bill lives in Halstead, Kansas with his two teenage children, who are the inspiration behind many of his stories. You can learn more about Bill at www.billbushauthor.com.

More information:
www.snaderpublishing.com

When the Time is Right

Halstead Mysteries 1

BILL BUSH

Halstead Mysteries 1: When the Time is Right
published by Snader Publishing Company, Halstead, Kansas, USA
This book is also available as eBook.

First published 2020

© 2020, all rights remain with the author
© 2020, cover design by Katharina Kolata, Independent Bookworm
© 2018, cover background by Katharina Kolata, Independent Bookworm
© 2018, cover girl by deniscristo, Depositphotos
© 2018, cover hair by deniscristo, Depositphotos
© 2020, cover cat by OpenClipart-Vectors, Pixabay
© 2020, cat paws by Elionas, Pixabay

printed On-Demand Publishing LLC, 100 Enterprise Way, Suite A200, Scotts Valley, CA 95066, USA, www.kdp.com

ISBN-13 978-1-945871-17-7

More information can be found on the publisher's website:
http://www.snaderpublishing.com

This series is for my mom, Phyllis Roth Lewis,
who loved murder mysteries.

TABLE OF CONTENTS

Chapter 1

*E*den slipped between the table and high chair full of plates and uneaten pizza crust, tipping over the crushed red pepper shaker which spilled open on the floor. She quickly cleared tables four and seven, pocketing two whole dollars. Two unleashed children and a larger than normal customer who didn't understand narrow aisle courtesy delayed her return trip to the kitchen.

"Hey, can you get us more drinks?"

One of the four teenagers in booth nine, the cute one, held up an empty cup. She lifted the tub full of dirty dishes *as if* they couldn't see her hands were full. "I'll be right back."

Oh God, I smell like toilet backwash and probably look awful. She set the dishes on the counter and brushed her hair down with her hand. *They look like they live in Pleasantville and I, well...* She brushed her short hair again, this time taking pride in her half-shaven style. *What do I care what they think?*

She popped a mint into her mouth and refilled their drinks. "Two Dr. Peppers, a Pepsi, and a Mountain Dew," she recited, setting each glass on the table.

"You're new to Halstead." It was the cute one who had asked for the refills. His smooth, black hair flowed down to his shoulders, and his baby face made Eden wonder if he even shaved yet. The rest of his body was well-developed though. He wore a blue cap with a white 'H'. His tank top showed muscular arms and his shorts displayed large calves.

"Um, did you just move to Halstead?" he repeated.

She blushed, realizing she was checking him out instead of answering his question. "I'm just visiting," she managed, then hurried back to the kitchen.

"That's Lucas Walls," the smiling, blond-haired girl working the cash register told her. "All four boys just graduated. They're celebrating because their baseball team won sub-state to advance to the state tournament."

The blond was petite and pretty. The four boys were clean cut and well groomed.

Eden fidgeted with one of the two ear-piercings she wore on each side, thankful to have left the others out. She started to slide her hand down as she thought of the dice tattooed on her neck, but stopped herself. She chastised herself for worrying about what anyone in this town thinks.

"Eden, can I talk to you for a minute?" the manager asked. His round face and body reminded her of BB-8.

Eden's eyes met concern in the cashier's as she followed the manager away from the crowd.

"I noticed you gave refills to the four high school boys in the other room." He rubbed the back of his neck. Was he going to say something about her tattoo? "We charge for refills. And typically we let them come to the counter to pay before giving them more to drink."

Eden clenched her teeth. They'd given free refills at her job last year at On the Border so she'd assumed the Pizza Parlor also did.

Apparently her manager read her mind. "Don't worry about it. Those boys are in here a lot and know better. They were just taking advantage of the newbie."

"I'm sorry," she managed, her ears still burning.

He chuckled. "I said don't worry about it. It's part of the learning curve."

"Order's ready," a voice rang from the kitchen.

"You're doing fine, Eden," the manager assured her. "Why don't you deliver those meals?"

Eden hurried to the kitchen to pick up two plates, one with spaghetti and garlic bread and one with a sandwich, chips and a long pickle.

The aroma streamed from the plate to Eden's nose and her stomach raged in protest. She had been too nervous to eat prior to her shift and now she suffered the consequences.

"Those go to table eight," the girl at the register informed her.

She glanced at the table map pinned to the wall and grunted. Table eight was next to the four boys. Ugh!

The line to order wove past the soda fountain, salad bar, and out the front door. Eden slipped through the crowd to the first dining room. *Were all Friday nights this busy?*

She passed the boys, determined not to make eye contact. Her foot caught and she stumbled forward, losing control of both plates. She landed hard on the ground with a thud and the glass plates cracked on contact. Laughter erupted from booth nine.

Except one boy wasn't laughing—Lucas.

"You stupid b—! You idiot!"

The dining room went silent.

He had the audacity to call her a bitch? Sure, he had stopped himself, but everyone in the restaurant knew what he meant.

She wanted to take a swing at him but had landed awkwardly on her side. The thin carpet had offered little cushion. What a klutz!

He was right, though. It was all her fault. Could she hide under the table? That wouldn't help, but maybe she could make a run for it.

He shook his leg and spaghetti flew off his foot and landed on her arm. "These are brand new Nikes!"

She reached to wipe the spaghetti sauce off of his shoes.

He slapped her arm away. "Don't touch me!"

She glared at him. He had no right to talk to her like that.

Someone behind Eden gasped.

Someone else shouted, "Lucas, your mom's going to hear about this!"

He didn't look back as he stormed away. "Let's go guys."

The other three boys shared uncertain glances, and one looked at her remorsefully, but when the two scurried out of the restaurant, he followed. Eden's anger burned, but she kept her head down. She heard the manager scolding them as they left, but she busied herself with cleaning up the mess, doing her best to ignore them and the other diners.

She fought back tears as she scooped noodles, meatballs, and the insides of a ham and cheese sandwich back onto the plates. The flat carpet would have to be shampooed to remove the sauce stain already setting in. Eden raced the ruined food back to the kitchen. Then she bolted out the back door and slammed her fist against the metal maintenance shed. Pain shot through her hand and up her arm.

She should have been at Disney World celebrating high school graduation with her two best friends instead of in this godforsaken dump.

Her face and ears flushed, but she refused to cry.

Her hand bled and ached, so she kicked the shed several times. The dents she made blended in with previous hail damage or other employee outbursts. She slumped to the ground and gave in to her tears. How could her new job have started any worse?

The manager stepped outside. "I told Lucas he wasn't welcome here for a while and that I was going to talk to his parents."

Talk to his parents? That sure wouldn't happen in the big city. "Thank you," she said half-heartedly.

"Accidents happen. What he said to you was unacceptable. His parents are good people. Lucas used to be a nice kid; I'm not sure what's gotten into him recently."

When Eden didn't say anything, he rubbed the back of his neck and continued. "I know you're upset, so take a couple of minutes to collect yourself, but then we need you back in there. We are extra busy tonight."

Eden hated herself. If she hadn't fallen she wouldn't be sitting outside, humiliated and alone. The guilt was familiar. Even though the judge had berated her, the court-appointed lawyer had been pleased. "You're fortunate. This is a good deal." Her lawyer was an idiot. The judge was an arrogant bastard. And Lucas was a bully! Soon the overwhelming guilt turned to anger. Whew! Anger she could live with, but not the guilt.

She could quit the job, but her probation agreement required her to live with her grandma for the summer. Jobs, especially for teenagers, were scarce in Halstead. So against her own wishes, Eden marched back into the Pizza Parlor.

As she finished washing her hand and snotty face, the tall cook immediately handed her a plate of spaghetti and another with a sandwich.

Déjà vu.

"This is the replacement for the ones you…uh, that were dropped."

Eden trudged back out to table eight, this time without the tripping or the annoying boys sitting at table nine. She swore everyone's eyes were glued on her to see if she would do a repeat performance.

She set the plates in front of the couple, an older couple of at least fifty. "I'm so sorry it took so long."

"That's okay, dear," the woman said with a smile. "We're in no hurry. What that boy said to you was horrible."

Eden dropped her head. The man started in on his spaghetti, but the lady put her hand on Eden's arm. Eden looked up and saw a pair of the kindest, most sympathetic eyes staring back at her. "I don't think I've seen you before. Are you new in town?"

Eden was relieved to change the subject. "Yes."

"What's your name?" the lady asked.

"Eden Price."

"Eden! What a unique name. I love it. I'm Stephanie Emmet, and the rude old man across from me is Doctor Roger Emmet."

Dr. Emmet continued eating.

"He's retired. He used to work at the hospital. We liked Halstead, so when the hospital closed we decided to retire instead of starting over elsewhere. Did you move here with your parents?"

"I'm just here for the summer, staying with my grandma."

"Oh, what's your grandma's name?"

"Marcia Murphy."

Mrs. Emmet's eyes rolled up in thought. "No, I don't think I know her."

"She moved here a few years ago, after my grandpa died," Eden explained. "She likes the small town and quiet neighborhood."

Eden stepped aside to allow a thirty-ish year old woman pass by with a plate full of salad. *Even the salad looked delicious.* She eyed it for several seconds before Eden stepped forward and focused her attention back to Mrs. Emmet.

"Well, welcome to Halstead. And if you ever need anything, we live on Washington, across the street from the hospital in a two-story brown house. In fact, why don't you come by tomorrow afternoon? I would love to visit with you and your grandma."

What a wonderful gesture. No, no, she shouldn't. She wasn't in town to make friends. "I'm sorry, but I have to work tomorrow."

"Surely not all day. Will you be done by four?"

She wasn't making this easy. A baby screamed in a nearby booth and Eden paused to think up an excuse. "I don't know what my grandma's schedule is."

"Well, if she can't make it then it'll just be the two of us. I'll have some snacks and tell you all you need to know to survive the summer in Halstead."

It *would* be nice to get some insight. Eden considered making up another excuse, but Mrs. Emmet was too nice to refuse. "Sure, sounds nice."

"Then I'll see you at four."

"Thank you." She noticed the doctor was almost finished. "I'd better let you eat."

She flipped her hand upward in dismissal. "Oh, he's used to waiting for me. It was nice to meet you."

Before Eden turned, the doctor gently grabbed her arm, slipped a twenty-dollar bill in her hand and closed her fingers around it. "Don't spend this."

Eden looked at the doctor, perplexed.

His eyes were wide and determined. "Read it when the time is right."

"Oh, Roger," Mrs. Emmet scolded. "He means spend it when the time is right."

"I—I—this is too much," Eden stuttered.

Doctor Emmet let go of her hand, stabbed a meatball, and shoved it in his mouth.

"Nonsense. We insist," Mrs. Emmet said. "Besides, Roger's the most stubborn man I know. You'd never be able to give that back to him."

"Thank you."

On her way back to the kitchen she glanced again at the twenty-dollar bill. Wow. She stuffed it in her pocket and finished her shift.

Eden stopped at her grandma's front door and huffed.

She wiped blood, once again, on her jeans. Everyone wore holes in their jeans; what was a little blood stain?

The blood had soaked through her bandage. She'd nearly screamed herself silly when she'd been cleaning the bathroom and bleach got into her cuts. Now it wouldn't stop bleeding. At least she wasn't going to die from chlorine poisoning.

Although the Pizza Parlor closed at nine it was nearly ten before Eden arrived at her grandma's house.

She swiped at a moth that dipped down from the porch light and crossed her face.

Stepping inside, the strong smell of coffee tempted her taste buds and she couldn't help but smile. Maimeo never drank coffee at night; said it kept her awake. She had made it for Eden.

Eden got an even greater surprise when she saw the plate of homemade peanut butter cookies in the center of the table. She wanted to shove every cookie in her mouth.

Maimeo was the best, but she often overreacted. As she shot out of her chair faster than Eden thought a seventy-one year-old could, Eden fought rolling her eyes. In her haste, Maimeo kicked the card table and several puzzle pieces ended up on the floor. She didn't seem to notice.

She tenderly examined Eden's bandage. "What happened, Peaches?"

Maimeo's nickname for Eden since her peaches-loving toddler years. Eden had outgrown it years ago. Maimeo hadn't. She pulled her hand away and grabbed a cookie. "It's nothing."

Her grandmother hustled her into the bathroom, cleaned and bandaged it properly. She reluctantly agreed that Eden didn't need stitches, which relieved Eden because she wanted cookies and coffee, not a trip to the emergency room.

Maimeo insisted on making a sandwich when she heard Eden's stomach growl. Of course, the food would cost her.

"Small straight." Maimeo wrote thirty on her Yahtzee score sheet.

Eden had devoured the sandwich and started to relax. Now that her hunger was tamed, she noticed other things like how much her feet and legs ached, that Maimeo had a new dish towel—probably homemade—with an owl in a tree embroidered on it, and the ticking of the wall clock. She might have to endure the Pizza Parlor all summer, but at least she had Maimeo's house to retreat to between shifts.

She bit off her coffee-soaked cookie and rolled. She rolled two more times and wrote nine in the three's column.

"How was work, dear?"

We charge for refills. Lucas and his friends had taken advantage of her. She shoved the thought from her mind.

"Good."

"Were the people you worked with nice?"

You stupid... his words echoed through her mind and Eden tensed. She thought of her manager and the friendly girl at the cash register.

"Yes."

"Did you make any new friends?"

These are brand new Nikes! Eden saw herself grabbing his foot and ripping it right off of his leg.

She gritted her teeth. "No."

At least the manager had barred Lucas from coming to the restaurant for a while. Hopefully for the rest of the summer. If BB-8 let him come back before that she would just quit. She didn't care what the judge would do to her.

"Eden Grace Price, what is going on?"

Her grandmother's stern voice brought her focus back to the present.

"I'm sorry, Maimeo."

Her grandmother retrieved the pot of coffee and re-filled Eden's cup, then poured herself one. "Why don't you tell me about it?"

Her hand prevented her from pretending nothing happened and she had never been able to lie to her grandma.

"It's a retarded boy."

"Eden! Calling someone retarded is a very disrespect-ful way to refer to a person with mental challenges."

Maimeo was right, but Eden laughed. "Actually, comparing them to Lucas Walls was disrespectful to the mentally disabled and I'll gladly apologize to every one of them."

Maimeo gaped at her and said nothing.

Eden told her everything, including how she had gotten angry and hit the shed behind the Pizza Parlor.

Her grandma leaned forward, took her hand and squeezed. "I'm so sorry, Peaches."

She was so sincere, Eden relaxed and smiled. "I know. It'll be fine. Lucas isn't allowed back at the Pizza Parlor and I don't plan to do much other than work, so hopefully I won't see him again."

"I don't know how to tell you this."

Eden pulled away from Maimeo, frightened that she wasn't making eye contact. "Tell me what?"

"Peaches, the Walls' live next door."

"Dough, sauce, cheese, mushrooms, onions, meat," Eden mumbled. "Dough, sauce, cheese, mushrooms, onions, meat." She slid the supreme pizza into the oven and started on the next one. "Dough, sauce, cheese, pepperonis."

"Eden, can you bus tables?" the manager barked from the cash register.

She gladly welcomed an escape from the monotony of making pizzas. Using a towel to wipe pizza sauce from her hands and her official employee t-shirt—oh well, it wasn't going to stay new for long anyhow—Eden grabbed a tub.

The Saturday lunch crowd was busier than the dinner crowd the night before. For three hours Eden bounced from making pizzas to bussing tables to washing dishes.

Her manager's name was Toby and the nice girl at the register was Ashley. She would work on learning more names later.

As the crowd thinned, Toby had Eden watch Ashley to learn how to work the front. Ashley explained how to answer the phone and to write for orders.

When they got a moment's break, Ashley asked her, "How are you doing? It's a lot to take in the first couple of days."

"Fine, I guess," Eden said unconvincingly. "Everyone's been nice. Well, almost everyone."

"Lucas is pretty convinced he's God's gift to mankind. Toby talked to his parents so I don't think you'll see him in here for a while." She paused a moment. "Has anyone invited you to church yet? You can come with me if you like."

Ugh! She would really have to interact with people if she went to church. "No thanks. I don't believe in God."

The front door opened, saving Eden from further explanation, and two police officers in dark blue uniforms entered. The younger of the two looked only a few years older than Eden. The older one stood several inches taller, wore a mustache, and looked much more at ease than his younger counterpart. They approached the counter. "Hi Ashley."

"Hi Officer Dirks. I think your order's ready." Ashley pulled two paper bags from the counter behind them that separated the front from the kitchen. She set them in front of the officers.

Toby exited the kitchen and joined Ashley and Eden behind the counter, wiping his hands on a towel. "No buffet today?"

"No, no time," Officer Dirks said. "Has Dr. Emmet been in here today?"

"He came in last night with his wife," Eden offered.

"But not today?" he asked Eden.

She shook her head.

"Is something wrong?" Toby asked, concerned.

"Mrs. Emmet is all worked up. She hasn't seen him since last night. Said he never came home."

Toby tossed the towel into a tub as the busboy passed. "Sometimes I see him out walking in the mornings, but now that I think about it, I didn't see him this morning."

"Well, it's probably nothing. Hopefully he'll turn up soon." He held up the bags. "In the meantime, we have to eat on the run."

When Eden's lunch shift concluded at three-thirty, she sat on the wooden bench in front of the Pizza Parlor until Maimeo arrived. She quickly explained what the police had said about Mrs. Emmet.

"I don't think we should bother her." Surely Mrs. Emmet wouldn't want company with her husband missing.

"I agree that she won't want company, but you told her you would be there and it would be rude not to show. Besides, maybe her husband has come home."

"But…"

Maimeo patted her knee and stood. "If he hasn't, we'll wish her well and politely excuse ourselves."

She still didn't want to go, but her grandma was right. They didn't have any other way to contact her so they should go.

They started toward the hospital in search of Mrs. Emmet's house. Between the hospital and the Pizza Parlor on Main Street were the fire station, police station, and city building, where the electronic sign displayed 89 degrees. The humidity made it feel several degrees hotter. In spite of the heat, Eden saw several walkers on the short stroll.

The hospital looked large in the middle of town but would have been dwarfed by the hospitals in Wichita. They approached the front of the hospital, then took the sidewalk along the north side. A walking path led from a side entrance of the hospital to a statue of an angel between two benches. In spite of its abandonment, the lawn remained well-manicured and the area designed for solitude maintained a sense of serenity.

A lone black SUV with red stripes in the parking lot provided the only signs of potential life.

It was an odd sight, seeing such a large building in the middle of a small town sitting empty.

Eden and her grandma turned down a curved road with the hospital emergency entrance on one side of the street displaying a six-foot wide emergency entrance sign, and large, two-story homes on the other. In the middle of the block stood a two-toned brown house with shutters around the windows. Rose bushes in full bloom—red, white, pink, yellow—lined the front entrance. The front yard was treeless, but a large maple towered over the house from the back yard.

They followed the steps onto the walk-around porch, complete with a corner gazebo. Eden desperately wanted to leave.

Oh, God! Hopefully Mrs. Emmet would put on a good front. If she cried, well; Eden hurriedly rang the doorbell before she changed her mind and fled.

No answer. Oh, well. Maybe Mrs. Emmet was asleep or didn't want to answer. At least they could say they tried.

Before she turned to leave, Mrs. Emmet opened the storm door and forced a smile. She wiped her red eyes with a tissue and immediately Eden felt horrible for intruding. Somehow, Mrs. Emmet maintained her hospitable attitude. "Oh, Eden. It's so good to see you. This must be your grandma. I'm Stephanie Emmet."

Mrs. Emmet stepped outside and let the storm door shut.

"Marcia Murphy." Maimeo took Mrs. Emmet's hands. "We can reschedule our visit, but we wanted to say how sorry we are and if there is anything you need, Eden and I want to be here for you."

Mrs. Emmet gave a genuine half smile then pulled one hand away to wipe her eyes.

They walked to the top step.

Mrs. Emmet leaned against the post as if she couldn't support her own weight any longer. "Thank you for understanding. I do want to visit with both of you, but until Roger is returned…"

"Is returned? You think someone took him?" Eden realized as soon as the words escaped her mouth she shouldn't have said them, especially with such shock. This was none of her business and would only upset Mrs. Emmet further. Maimeo's glare said that she agreed.

"Yes, he was kidnapped…" She buried her face in her tissue and blew, her arms shaking uncontrollably.

Eden was stunned. Someone kidnapped? In this little town?

Mrs. Emmet blew her nose again and Eden feared she might cry, or worse, want to talk. Thankfully, Mrs. Emmet stepped toward her house and when Eden held the storm door open, she retreated inside.

Maimeo gave her a hug before stepping away. "I'm sorry. If there's anything we can do, please ask."

"Thank you," Mrs. Emmet managed before she shut the front door.

You sure know how to make friends, Eden thought as she strode down the porch steps.

Eden propped her feet on the footstool and glided easily back and forth. Maimeo had said the glider was designed for mothers of newborns, but they didn't have them when she was a young mother so she was getting her use of it now.

She tilted her head back to look up through the sunroof. Maimeo had enclosed and renovated her back porch two years ago. The room still smelled of new cedar.

The stars had yet to appear, but would soon light up the sky. Eden loved the view. Maimeo lived on the edge of town, which meant very little light interference. Not that there was an overwhelming amount of light anywhere in town; not compared to Wichita.

She couldn't get the image of Mrs. Emmet, shaking and sobbing, out of her mind. She had been so nice to Eden the night before, when she had especially needed it after Lucas had blasted her in public. She wanted to do something nice, but didn't know what. You don't send flowers to someone whose husband has been kidnapped, do you?

Her grandmother had gone to bed and Eden sat alone in the back room.

She watched a couple of funny cat videos on Youtube—boy were cats stupid—then tossed her phone onto the loveseat after the third video kept freezing. She always struggled with reception in Halstead. She had the wrong carrier for this dump of a town.

She picked up her book, but her mind wandered back to Mrs. Emmet. Usually Eden was good at ignoring pain, her own as well as that of others. She didn't like helping people with their emotional messes. She didn't have many friends because *everybody* had an emotional mess.

Books allowed her to enter a world to experience the worst and the best of people without the messiness of relationships. Those were the kind of emotions Eden liked.

Her book remained closed as her mind wandered. The glider went forward and backward, forward and backward. She slowly closed her eyes and let her body relax.

Bright lights startled her awake. The clear sound of a car engine through the opened window drew her attention. Headlights slid across the alley and a red convertible parked on the concrete slab next door. The car door opened and a tall boy dressed in jeans and a dark shirt stepped out.

Eden reached over and turned off the lamp, leaving her in complete darkness. She crouched near the window like a secret agent or a spy.

Was that who she thought it was? She threw her book in frustration. It was! She had tried hard to believe he didn't really live next door.

Lucas hustled into the white shed and came out with a large bag weighted on his shoulder. He opened the trunk of the shiny red car and tossed the bag in. Eden gasped. She could have sworn something moved. Lucas doubled over like he had been hit in the gut. This gave Eden a clear view. A blanket inside the trunk moved; someone was wrapped in it, struggling to get out. Lucas punched the blanket, then slammed the trunk shut. He quickly got into the car and sped away.

Eden ran out the back and tried to follow but there was no way to keep up. She didn't own a car. What could she have done anyway?

She returned to the back porch and curled up in a ball on the loveseat. So much for a nice quiet summer. Not only had someone been kidnapped, but the neighbor who hated her guts had done the kidnapping. She was no longer comfortable in her little slice of paradise.

Eden found Maimeo's home phone and dialed 9-1-1.

Chapter 2

Officer Dirks spent an hour with Eden making her repeat her story over and over and over again. After she had repeated it for the umpteenth time, she decided he was stalling until Lucas returned home.

Of course, he said every detail was important and wanted to make sure she hadn't missed something. He was skeptical that Lucas had Dr. Emmet in the trunk of his car. Eden didn't want to believe it either, but she had seen it.

Finally, Officer Dirks left to search for Lucas.

Maimeo had supported her; stood up for her when Officer Dirks doubted her story.

They had been up for several hours, so after giving her a kiss on the forehead, her grandma returned to bed.

Eden exhaled, relieved to be alone. She thought of Lucas hitting Dr. Emmet then slamming the trunk shut. She quickly locked the doors and pushed furniture in front of them. She turned on most of the lights in the house, and held tightly to her phone. It was overkill, she knew, and no wonder that sleep eluded her.

Around eight the next morning she made herself a pot of coffee and began feeding her body the caffeine she would need to make it through her lunch shift at work.

She pushed the loveseat away from the back door. She returned the coffee table to its original spot and opened the front door for a breath of fresh air, and gasped. Lucas, wearing knit shorts and a Halstead Dragons t-shirt, casually tossed a baseball to the young officer who had been in the Pizza Parlor yesterday. The oddity of a uniformed policeman wearing a baseball mitt and playing catch quickly lost its intrigue.

What about the body?

For several moments Eden stared in disbelief. The officer stood ten feet from the red Mustang, playing a kid's game and jovially chatting with the kidnapping suspect. Was the trunk empty? Why wasn't he interrogating Lucas about what it had contained the night before? Occasionally, they laughed and Eden's anger boiled. The officer should be arresting Lucas, not joking with him.

As he wound up, Lucas caught sight of Eden and stopped. The policeman turned in her direction before she slammed the door.

What's happening? Lucas must have disposed of the body. That meant it was her word against his.

She peered out the window. Lucas and the officer clasped hands and gave each other a semi-hug. She quickly locked the door and leaned back against it.

When someone pounded on the door, she startled. What if Lucas had come to silence her? She'd probably seen too many horror movies. This was small town America, right?

She couldn't pretend not to be home, not after they had seen her.

Her grandma entered the living room, feet dragging. "What's with all the noise?"

"I'm sorry, Maimeo."

Another loud knock.

"Who is it?" Eden yelled.

"Officer Johnson, ma'am."

Ma'am? She didn't know if anger, fear, or discouragement kept her from wanting to talk to Officer Johnson.

"Don't just stand there, dear. Let him in." Maimeo shooed her away from the door.

"I'm Mickey Johnson of the Halstead Police Department." He stuck out his hand.

Eden's eyes went from Officer Johnson's face to his hand twice. She couldn't make her arm move; didn't want to shake hands anyway. She tried to apologize but her throat caught. Remaining quiet seemed the safest move.

Maimeo grabbed his hand and shook. "I'm Marcia Murphy and this rude girl is my granddaughter, Eden Price. Can I get you a cup of coffee?"

"No ma'am. Thank you." He looked at Eden. "I'm following up on your report from last night. We searched the suspect's trunk and found it empty. Clean, in fact. No evidence that anyone had been inside."

None? But…but…of course! Lucas must have cleaned up thoroughly to rid his car of evidence. He must have acted quickly, though. "Wh-when did you search?"

"About an hour ago, ma'am."

"So he had all night to clean the trunk before you searched it?"

He adjusted his cap. "Well, yes, ma'am."

Was he that polite? It was too much. "So he could have had a body in the trunk last night, disposed of it, and removed any traces?"

"Look ma'am…"

"It's Eden."

"Okay, Eden. I know Lucas, and he would never have a body in his trunk."

"Look, Officer Johnson. If Eden says she saw a body in the trunk, then she saw it."

"I'm sorry. I'm only telling you what we found, or didn't find."

She knew her face had turned red; she could feel it burn. She'd seen a body and this buffoon couldn't tell her differently. "Did you interrogate him?"

"We asked him several questions. He said he spent the night at a friend's house and his friend corroborated his story. I'm sorry, I thought you'd like—"

Eden shut the door. She didn't want to hear any more.

Two cups of coffee, half a can of Mountain Dew, and a nice, long shower energized her. Some blush, eye shadow, and glossy lip balm helped her feel presentable for the public.

She cracked the front door; the coast was clear. The air was warm and humid. She thought the clouds to the east looked promising. Rain would either cool things off or spike the humidity. You never knew.

She didn't make it out of the yard before she heard Lucas.

"What's wrong with you? Calling the police?"

"The police told you I was the one who reported you?" Surely they weren't allowed to do that. Weren't they supposed to protect informants?

"They didn't have to. They were at your house last night and this morning. It's obvious you called them because I yelled at you. Did I hurt your *feelings*?" He used his best baby voice for the last question.

He had a lot of nerve making fun of her after what he'd said to her at the Pizza Parlor.

She knew she should ignore him, but against her better judgment, she spun on her heels. Eden didn't care much for people, and she hated confrontation. But she was pissed.

"Did the police ask you about Dr. Emmet?"

Lucas tossed a navy blue duffle bag into the trunk but held the silver Easton bat over his shoulder. "What?"

"Did you take him?"

Lucas scoffed. "I don't even know the old doctor."

"I saw you last night. I know you had a body in your trunk."

"Yeah, I had Dr. Emmet stuffed in my trunk."

"I knew it!"

"That was sarcasm, moron." He slammed the trunk shut, bat still in hand.

Eden took a step back. "You can't hide from the truth."

He pointed the bat in her direction. "If you think I kidnapped Dr. Emmet, prove it."

Another step back. "That's not my job."

"Whatever!" He opened his car door.

She had one more thing she needed to know. Half a step forward. "How do you know Officer Johnson?"

Lucas swung the bat toward where the police car had been parked. "You mean Mickey?"

Eden's voice was accusatory. "You call him Mickey?"

Lucas beamed. "Officer Johnson is my cousin. We grew up together. We were talking about the Royals game we went to last week."

"Oh." Crap. She hadn't seen that coming. But that would explain the game of catch and the friendly hug.

Lucas rose to another level of arrogance. "If you like, I can call Mickey, um, I mean Officer Johnson. You can show him the evidence you have that I kidnapped Dr. Emmet and kept him in the trunk of my car last night. Oh! But that's right—you don't have any proof."

He got into his car and sped away.

Eden growled through gritted teeth, "I don't have any proof... *yet.*"

Chapter 3

On her way to work, Eden's anger gave way to reason. She had given the police a solid lead and eventually they would trace Lucas to Dr. Emmet's disappearance. But how? They hadn't found any evidence.

Wait! Maybe that was it! What if Officer Johnson helped with the crime? Or was covering it up for his cousin? She entered the Pizza Parlor through the back entrance, slipped through the kitchen and clocked in. She hadn't noticed the kitchen crew, her manager Toby who wished her a good morning, or Ashley who was thirty seconds into her monologue when Eden realized she was talking.

"…but do you think I should have kept my mouth shut?"

"Huh?"

Ashley put her hands on her hips. "Eden! Did you hear a thing I said?"

"I, uh…no. I'm sorry, Ashley. I have a lot on my mind."

"Is Lucas still giving you a hard time?" The phone rang. "Eden, you have phone duty," Toby called from the kitchen.

"I'll tell you when it slows down." She made a grab for the phone. "This is The Pizza Parlor. Eden speaking. How may I help you?"

Two and a half hours later the line to order subsided. The waves of the church crowd had dissipated long ago, but many remained in the restaurant and casually visited. Although the restaurant remained crowded, the employees relaxed and focused on cleanup.

Eden grabbed a tub and dishcloth and helped Ashley clear four tables that had been pushed together. "I need to find out what happened to Dr. Emmet. But I don't want to ask Mrs. Emmet and upset her."

"I heard my parents talk about it last night. My dad said Dr. Emmet went to the hospital Friday night to work and he never came home. The next morning Mrs. Emmet woke up alone. She searched the hospital and when she didn't find him she became frantic and called the police."

"He works at the hospital? I thought it was closed."

Eden held up a clear plastic cup that contained some sort of mixture that included ketchup, grated cheese, and a french fry. She made a disgusted face and Ashley laughed.

"Dad said Dr. Emmet has a lab there. He does research for a medical company in Wichita."

The door dinged and Mrs. Emmet entered. She wore a smile and looked much more like the woman Eden had met two days ago than the one she saw yesterday.

"Hello, Mrs. Emmet." Eden met her at the register and picked up a pen. "What can I get for you?"

"I'm not here to eat, dear. I was hoping we could reschedule our tea. I would like to make up for missing yesterday."

"I'd like that."

Mrs. Emmet brushed her curly bangs from her eyes. "I'm sorry I was such a mess yesterday. When Roger vanished it upset me. It still does, but I had a good night's sleep and woke up realizing there isn't anything I can do about it."

"That's okay," Eden assured her. "Anyone would have been upset. I hope the police find your husband soon."

They agreed on four o'clock that afternoon and Mrs. Emmet turned to leave, but Eden had a thought and caught her before she reached the door. "Mrs. Emmet, does your husband know Lucas Walls?"

"Not well. But yes, I think he said one time that he paid Lucas to do a few odd jobs for him. Why do you ask?"

Eden hesitated. "I don't trust him. Did you see Lucas at the hospital Friday evening?"

Mrs. Emmet shook her head. "The only person I saw outside the hospital was Sam. Maybe he saw Lucas."

"Who is Sam?"

"I really must be going. I'll see you at four." Mrs. Emmet hurriedly left the restaurant.

Eden shot a quick text to her grandmother telling her about the new tea time with Mrs. Emmet.

"What was that all about?" Ashley asked Eden when she returned to the counter.

Eden glanced around the room as if a spy might be listening. She spoke as quietly as she could. "Last night I saw something move in the trunk of Lucas's car. What if it was Dr. Emmet?"

This time when Ashley slapped her hands over her mouth it didn't come across as too dramatic. "Do you really think it was? Are you sure something moved? You should call the police."

"Yes, I'm positive I saw something move. I even saw Lucas punch him. And I did call the police, but I guess one of the police officers is Lucas's cousin."

"Do you think the police are in on it?"

"Maybe. Or maybe Officer Johnson isn't taking it seriously because he knows Lucas. Either way, nothing happened."

A couple left so Eden grabbed a tub to clean the table and Ashley followed.

Eden cleaned; Ashley talked. "What are you going to do?"

Eden shrugged. "What can I do?"

"You could figure out what Lucas did with Dr. Emmet."

"The police are investigating."

"Are they?"

Eden didn't want to do anything that might mean running into Lucas again. So why did she feel the need to do something?

"Think of Mrs. Emmet. Can you ignore this when she is hurting so much?"

And this is why Eden tried not to get close to people. "Okay, I'm going to prove that Lucas took Dr. Emmet."

Ashley nearly jumped for joy. "How are you going to do it?"

Eden dumped the tub in the kitchen and followed Ashley to the salad bar. They wiped up splattered salad dressing, pudding, and spilled sunflower seeds as she continued.

"I don't know, but Mrs. Emmet said she thought Lucas did some work for Dr. Emmet. She also said Sam might have seen Lucas at the hospital the night the doctor disappeared. I guess I could start with Sam. Maybe he saw something that would be useful. Do you know him?"

"Sam Nelson's a drunk. My mom's convinced he's going to drink himself to death."

"So you *do* know him?" Eden said enthusiastically.

Ashley shook her head adamantly. "No. But he walks around town, drunk. A lot. Everyone knows who he is."

Eden retrieved more crackers and bacon bits while Ashley got lettuce, Ranch dressing, and shredded cheese from the fridge.

"In case I don't get lucky enough to catch him roaming around town, I need to find out where he lives."

"Oh, I can tell you that," Ashley volunteered. "He lives a few houses down from my best friend on Adams Street. Go south on Main, four blocks. Take a left on Adams. It's the smallest house on the block, an old, white, rundown place. I'll go with you when we get off, if you want."

Eden wiped the drops of Ranch Ashley spilled as she refilled the container. "Thanks, but I couldn't ask you to do that."

"I would love to. It's so exciting; investigating a real case!"

"I appreciate it, but I can't let you go with me to a drunk's house. What would your parents say?"

Ashley's bowed head told Eden what she already knew. Ashley's parents were strict and there was no way they would want their sixteen-year-old visiting Sam.

They returned the salad bar supplies to the kitchen.

"I want to help. Is there something I can do?" Ashley persisted.

"I don't know—"

"Please!"

Eden thought. "Okay. You've lived here all your life; probably know lots of people. Ask whoever you can and find out about Officer Johnson. I need to know what kind of person he is. Is he trustworthy? Is he honest? What kind of character does he have? I need to figure out if he's involved or not. Do you think you can do that?"

Ashley beamed. "You won't be disappointed."

Immediately when Eden got off work she walked south on Main Street. She checked her phone. Maimeo had returned her text. She thought it was great that Mrs. Emmet was up for company, but she had a ladies Bible study at four. Ugh!

Lucas had lied to her. He had told her he didn't know the doctor, but Mrs. Emmet said he had done work for her husband. He was hiding something. Why else would he unless he had kidnapped Dr. Emmet? Maybe Sam had seen him.

Ashley was right, Eden easily found the small house. The overgrown yard and the screen door hanging by one hinge testified of Sam's neglect, and she was sure she could smell alcohol before she even reached his yard.

Approaching the alcoholic's door, the odor, it was all familiar.

Maybe that's why she didn't think twice about visiting this stranger while he was drinking—she might as well have been visiting her dad.

Eden knocked on the door. The television blared from inside. She pounded louder.

"Who is it?" a voice shouted above the television.

"My name's Eden!" How could he possibly hear her? She pounded on the door again. Almost immediately it sprang open and a wall of smoke hit her like the Sunday morning church crowd swarming The Pizza Parlor after services.

The man before her was frail and disgusting. He had a receding hairline, several days' facial growth, a white tank top that exposed protruding chest hair, and jeans. His stench begged for a shower, which he must have ignored for days.

"Who are you?" It was a demand, not a question.

"My name's Eden Price and I'm in town visiting my grandma, Marcia Murphy. I live in Wichita and am only here for the summer—"

"I don't want your whole damned life story. What do you want? You selling something? Because I don't buy crap just to make you kids happy." He retreated to his recliner as he spoke. On the far side of the chair stood an ashtray and on the nearside a television tray with eight empty beer bottles and a clear cigarette lighter that said *Absolut Vodka* in bold blue letters. He picked it up and lit a cigarette.

She hollered over the blaring television. "I'm not selling anything. Are you Sam Nelson?"

"Yeah." He motioned for her to come in, but she didn't budge. "Shut the door, for Christ's sake. Can't you see I got the air conditioner running?" He pointed to the window unit that blew noisily—surely the reason for the television being so loud.

She looked behind as if someone could advise her. It did feel nice and cool inside. She would never go into the house of someone she didn't know in Wichita, but everyone seemed friendlier and more laid back in Halstead. She stepped inside and closed the door. "I want to ask you some questions about last night."

Sam leaned far to his right, opened the refrigerator door, and pulled out a bottle of beer. He took a long drink. Her dad would be envious of a beer fridge in the living room. He'd also be a lot heavier.

Sam wasn't fat, though. In fact, if anything he looked too thin. Eden had heard about drunks that hardly ate and lived on beer. Sam must be in that category.

On the other side of the refrigerator was a lonely couch covered with a tattered blanket. Judging from the armrests, the blanket was there to cover stains.

The walls were bare. Papers, magazines, dishes, and beer bottles cluttered the floor, along with a few other items Eden couldn't identify.

Sam reached down and his hand disappeared underneath some newspapers. It reappeared moments later with a remote control. Finally, the volume on the television was lowered. "You talk too soft." Sure, it was *her* fault they couldn't hear each other.

"I said I want to ask you some questions about last night," Eden repeated. "Mrs. Emmet said you were outside the hospital."

"What the hell is it any of your business what I did last night? And sit down. You're making me nervous hovering there like that."

The last thing she wanted to do was get comfortable, but she needed information from him. She tentatively sat on the edge of the couch, keeping as little of her body in contact with it as possible. "I'm trying to figure out what happened to Dr. Emmet."

"I can tell you exactly what happened to him."

Bingo! She knew he had seen Lucas. "You know what happened to Dr. Emmet?"

"Sure I do!" He took a drink from his beer and another puff from his cigarette.

When he didn't volunteer the information, Eden asked, "What happened to him?"

"He's hiding."

"What do you mean, he's hiding?" Eden asked, suddenly confused.

"That no-good son of a bitch was my son's doctor. He killed my son, but he and his high-priced lawyers got the jury to side with them. He got away scot-free and I got a life without my son."

Well, crap! That was more than she wanted to know. Now what? "I'm so sorry about your son. What was his name?"

The bitter old man did something completely unexpected. His lip quivered and a tear ran down his cheek. It was followed by another and soon several more. "His name was Samuel," the drunk blubbered. "But…but we called him Shaggy… because he…he liked…he wanted to be Scooby-Doo's best friend." Sam wept bitterly.

Eden sat in uncomfortable silence. Her dad had mastered the art of crying on demand. As a child, he used his crying to manipulate her, so she built up a wall. It had been years since she'd allowed him to control her emotions. Sam's tears flowed genuinely, she had no doubt. More than once she thought about bolting out of there. Would there be a better time to question him though? He might not let her in a second time, so she waited for his emotions to run their course.

Instead of using a tissue from the box on the coffee table, which sat against the wall directly behind Sam's chair, he picked up a dirty white tank top from the floor and blew his nose. Eden gagged and could taste a little of the mushroom pizza she had for lunch.

"Shaggy was the last person I ever cared about."

"I'm sorry, but what does your son have to do with the doctor hiding?"

"It was twenty years ago tomorrow."

Wow! Suddenly Eden felt a wave of anger. It sucked when kids died. "Tomorrow's the anniversary?" she asked quietly.

Sam nodded. "Dr. Emmet probably left town because he knows that his negligence twenty years ago caused the death of my son and he doesn't want to face up to it."

That could be a reasonable explanation.

Eden was hesitant to ask the next question but knew she needed to get it cleared up—mark him off the list, so to speak. "So you didn't have anything to do with his disappearance?" She was relieved when he remained calm. In fact, he reclined in his chair until it was nearly horizontal. A cigarette still rested between his lips.

"No. Don't get me wrong. I hate the man and wish him dead. But I'd never do anything to him. It's not the job of one man to decide the fate of another. I'm sure everyone will think I had something to do with him being gone. I'll get the blame until he returns. But mark my words, he'll return. In the end I'll be proved right; he's just a coward." Sam's words were beginning to slur.

"I think someone took Dr. Emmet, but I don't think it was you. Did you see anyone at the hospital last night?"

"No. After I left the doctor's house I came home. I drank for a while and passed out."

"You were at the doctor's house?"

"Outside. Yelling at that gutless quack."

"Why?"

Sam pounded his chest. "Challenging him to come out and fight me like a man, the coward."

She changed direction. "Do you know Lucas Walls?"

Sam took the cigarette from his mouth and slowly pointed it at Eden. "Lucsas… Luscas… Luc Wallis." He squinted his eyes like he suddenly couldn't see her. He attempted one more time to pronounce Lucas's name before he passed out. The cigarette dropped from his dangling arm.

Eden shrieked and stomped it out, adding another burn mark to the carpet.

"Mr. Nelson? Mr. Nelson?" She wanted to shake him to make sure he was alive, but he was so gross. She took several tissues and used them to avoid direct contact. "Sam? Sam!"

He mumbled, but didn't move. He coughed a few times which made Eden jump back. Then he settled into a deep, loud snore.

"At least you aren't dead, old man." Eden waded through the pile of scattered newspapers toward the door, but stopped when her foot kicked something solid. She picked up a leather-bound book. There were no words or pictures on the front, just a simple brown cover. She opened it and saw writing. It was a journal.

She felt guilt creep up her spine, but a crudely drawn picture of a man hanging from a noose concerned her enough to read. The first couple of pages told a story about a patient who died but came back to life and killed the doctor. The next few pages contained a story about a doctor who was being haunted by the ghosts of all his former patients who had died. She quickly skimmed the next hundred pages or so. There were dozens of fictional tales about a doctor being haunted, beaten, and murdered by his patients. This Sam Nelson had issues.

She flipped pages until she found a page dated January 3, 2021.

Dear God, everyone says I'm a loser. They're all right! I am a loser, but it's not my fault it's yours. You allowed my son to die. You gave me this shitty body that's incapable of having sex; you let my wife run away. Now you've dumped me back in this hell hole so I have to see the doctor who killed Shaggy all the time. Who wouldn't be an alcoholic if they had to endure what I do. You suck!

She wanted to stop reading, but the next page caught her attention.

I don't know what the doctor is doing, but he's experimenting on animals. They took a goat into the hospital and left without it. I snuck into the hospital and looked around but couldn't find the goat anywhere. They must be dissecting the animals and doing something with their body parts, because I couldn't find evidence of a live animal anywhere in the hospital. I searched for hours.

Sam snorted and Eden jumped and squealed. She slammed her hand over her mouth and froze. Sam continued to snore. She wanted to leave, but Sam's journal enthralled her. Another grunt from Sam scared her enough to put the journal back where she found it and hustle away.

Chapter 4

*E*den quietly left Sam's house and started for home along the sidewalk. She had only gone a couple of blocks when she recognized the red Mustang, top down, driving her way. As Lucas approached, he slowed and turned the blaring music down. He revved the engine, but Eden continued a brisk pace with her eyes forward. He stopped and drove in reverse, keeping pace with her. "Hey, Wallflower!" Keep going. "Pigtail!" Ignore him. "Idiot!" I just want to kill him. "Hey b—"

"You have to be the most arrogant, pig-headed, annoying, stuck-up, low-life, rude, insignificant piece of trash I have ever met!" She leaned with both her arms on the passenger door. Her face burned and she certainly had spit during her tirade. "Everyone told me the people in a small town are so nice and friendly. 'By the time summer's over you'll feel like you're part of the big family of Halstead. Everyone's so down-to-earth and they all get along, not like in the big city.' Well, I'll tell you what. We have some stupid bastards in Wichita, some I wouldn't want to be alone with at night, but I would take any of them over you."

She took a deep breath. She hadn't been that winded since she'd had to run the mile in P.E. last month, which happened to be the last time she had exercised. She realized she was leaning against his car and quickly took a step back.

Whatever reaction he had expected from her, this clearly wasn't it. For the first time since she met Lucas, he was speechless.

"Now tell me, Lucas, God's gift to mankind, your highness, why did you lie to me?"

"What are you talking about?" He had tempered the anger in his voice, but it remained in his eyes.

"You told me you didn't know Dr. Emmet. Well, I had a talk today with Mrs. Emmet and she told me that you did some work for her husband. So why did you lie?"

"So what if I did a few errands for Dr. Emmet? What business is it of yours anyway?"

"It's my business because I am the one who saw you with a body in the trunk of your car last night. I think you had something to do with his disappearance and I aim to prove it."

Lucas laughed, surely to cover his nervousness.

Eden narrowed her eyes at him. "Where were you last night? What was in your trunk?"

"I don't have to tell you anything," he spat.

"Were you at the hospital?" she prodded.

He adjusted his rearview mirror.

Eden glanced behind him but no one was coming. *Was he stalling?*

"I told you I wasn't there and I didn't have anything to do with his disappearance."

"I don't believe you."

Lucas shifted in his seat, foot still on the brake, and stared at Eden. "I'm warning you, if you keep poking your nose into this you're going to find yourself deep into something you'll wish you stayed away from."

Eden started to lean into his car again but caught herself. "Are you threatening me?"

He turned his body forward again, his voice calm. "I'm telling you. You don't know what you're messing with."

He sped away so fast that Eden instinctively jumped back, lost her balance, and landed on her side in the middle of the street. *He could have run over my feet!* Other than the big scrape on her left arm, she was fine.

As she stood, she had a hunch, so instead of going home she walked to the hospital.

She circled it, thinking Lucas might be there. She didn't know why. A silly hunch, maybe. She wasn't a cop, so why did she think a hunch would work?

The same black SUV she had seen earlier remained parked in the circle drive at the front entrance. Eden wanted to see inside the building, to find Dr. Emmet's work area. She started with the front door and it opened.

How odd. The fully furnished lobby looked ready to host waiting patients. A hall with several doors extended from the lobby, one of them open with a light shining out.

She quietly approached the lighted doorway and peered in. The large room had a desk and guest chairs set up in the front third as a makeshift office. Behind the desk, carefully stacked boxes lined one wall and a counter with cupboards, drawers, and three Acer laptops sitting atop one another. Tall stacks of papers piled on the desk hid the small, thin lady sitting behind it. Eden saw her in the reflection of the picture of a tropical island on the wide wall. The lady typed away on her keyboard.

Eden dashed past the doorway, then briskly walked toward the door at the far end of the hallway.

"May I help you?"

Eden gulped. She'd hoped to make it cleanly by.

"I was just passing by and thought I would stop in to check out the hospital." She knew it wasn't a good lie.

The lady stood in the doorway with her arms crossed, glaring at Eden.

How could she secretly investigate? She stunk at sneaking around. "I'm a friend of Mrs. Emmet's and wanted to look at Dr. Emmet's lab for clues to where he's at."

"The police have already been here," the lady said curtly.

"Well, Mrs. Emmet is really worried and the police think he might not even be missing, that he went somewhere and just forgot to tell Mrs. Emmet. She's really worried. Did I mention that already?" Eden smiled shyly. "Where are my manners? My name is Eden Price." She approached the lady with the deathly stare and held out her hand.

"I'm Jessica Barnes, *if* you must know." Chills swept through Eden as their hands touched. Jessica's hand was as cold as her eyes. Maybe her whole body was cold. She wore black leggings, a long, thick T-shirt that hung to her thighs, and a light denim jacket; more clothing than most on a hot summer day inside a hospital without an air conditioner running. "This is not a public facility but a privately owned hospital."

"Privately owned? By who?"

"You ask a lot of questions that are none of your business. Now, Eden Price, let me explain this to you simply. You are trespassing. Consider this a courtesy warning, in case you missed the 'no trespassing' sign as you entered. You can scamper on out of here like a good little girl or I can call the police."

She *had* missed the sign. She lacked even the basic investigation skills. Eden started to say something but Jessica quickly cut her off. "Or you can ask one more question and I will physically remove you myself and tell the police you were belligerent. And in case you question my authority, I am the majority owner of the hospital and have every right to defend my property." Jessica held open one side of her jacket to reveal a pistol handle protruding from an inside pocket. "So please, say one more thing so I can confront your snotty little ass."

Eden ran.

Chapter 5

*E*den heard voices and followed them to the alley behind the hospital, where Lucas' red Mustang sat parked. She knew it! Her hunch had just been a little early. She used the row of hedges along the alley to get as near as she dared. She couldn't get close enough to see Lucas and the older gentleman—Eden surmised by his voice.

The sun cast the alley in the hospital's shadow. Eden didn't know for sure, but thought they stood in a loading dock area.

"It's imperative that no one finds out what really happened to the doctor," the man said quietly but emphatically.

"I understand." That was definitely Lucas's voice.

"You're going to get a lot of heat, but hang tough. There's no solid evidence against you and this will all blow over in a few days. If you keep to the story, I'll make it worth it for you and your family."

She heard feet shuffling and risked edging closer to the convertible.

She could now see Lucas. The other gentleman remained out of view, but she didn't dare move any closer. Lucas took a thick manila envelope from the man, reached in and pulled out what appeared to be a bundle of bills.

"That's the down payment. The police may come down on you hard, so go home and practice your story."

Eden ducked out of sight before Lucas returned to his car, tossed the envelope into the passenger's seat, and sped away.

Chapter 6

*E*den found the benches by the angel statue and took a seat. The sun burned bright on what already felt like a summer day. In thirty minutes she saw two joggers, three women pushing strollers, and a family of five riding their bicycles. Halstead residents liked their exercise. A light wind blew and the place felt as serene as it looked. A few minutes before four, Eden stood and stretched. She walked to Mrs. Emmet's brown house and rang the doorbell. She tensed when the doorknob turned. *What if Mrs. Emmet was upset again?*

Mrs. Emmet opened the storm door and smiled. "Eden, it's so good to see you. Please do come in."

Eden returned the smile and was shocked to realize that this was the first time since she'd arrived in Halstead that she felt truly welcome.

"I have tea and sandwiches in the living room."

Eden followed Mrs. Emmet past the spiral staircase into the front room with the large window. The room was decorated in the Victorian style, with furniture in pristine condition looking like it dated back two hundred years. Two cream-colored sofas and a matching chair horseshoed around a marble-topped coffee table. All four pieces, along with the two end tables on either side of the sofa, had matching trimmed wood, spectacular in detail.

Her grandmother sat on the couch, holding a beautiful, white quilt with purple flowers. "Hi Peaches!"

Maimeo set the perfectly folded quilt on the back of the sofa. Eden ran her finger along the outline of the petals.

"Hi Maimeo. I thought you had Bible study?"

"I do. When I heard Mrs. Emmet was up for company I decided to stop by before my study."

Maimeo gave her a hug. "I'll see you by ten."

It wasn't a question. She had strict rules set up, but Eden didn't care because she had no plans for a personal life this summer. Although it was good her grandmother didn't know about her visit to Sam's. "Yes, of course."

Mrs. Emmet escorted Maimeo to the door then returned.

Eden was still admiring the quilt. "Did you make this?"

"Heavens no. I don't have the patience for such a task. I bought it at a charity auction years ago. I just loved the flowers. Isn't it lovely?"

"It's gorgeous," Eden agreed.

"Where are you from, dear?" Mrs. Emmet poured a cup of tea from the platter that sat on the coffee table.

"I live in Wichita with my mom."

"Are you done with high school?" she asked.

Eden took a seat on the couch and held the warm cup. "Yes, I just graduated last week."

Mrs. Emmet took a drink. "How do you like Halstead so far?"

Eden hesitated to drink hot tea with sweat sitting on the back of her neck, but she took a sip to be polite. "It's a lot different than Wichita, that's for sure."

For the next hour and a half Eden and Mrs. Emmet had a wonderful visit. Mrs. Emmet asked all about Eden's life in Wichita and her future plans now that she had graduated, and told her all about her and Dr. Emmet's dating, marriage, and time in Halstead. Mrs. Emmet recalled fondly her dear Roger and only cried once.

Eden hadn't felt this relaxed since arriving in Halstead. Mrs. Emmet helped take her mind off of the last two days.

After three cups of tea and ninety minutes of conversation, Eden decided she had better leave. She didn't want to overstay her welcome.

"I'm so glad we had this time to visit," Mrs. Emmet said as she escorted Eden to the door. She followed Eden onto the porch. The sun had moved behind the large tree which now cast its shadow across the street and onto the hospital. "And it was nice to get my mind off of the last forty-eight hours and focus on pleasant things. Tell me, why did you ask if I had seen Lucas around the hospital Saturday evening?"

Eden didn't know what to say. The old man, whoever he was, knew where the doctor was, and so did Lucas. Or did he? Either way, Lucas had taken him. But she had no proof, and didn't want to say anything until she knew for sure. "Lucas lied to me, so I thought he might have something to do with Dr. Emmet's disappearance."

Mrs. Emmet didn't say anything and Eden shifted awkwardly.

"You are doing much better. Have you heard from your husband?"

"No." She paused. "Lucas is just a kid. I don't know if he's capable of something like you're suggesting."

"I hope not, but he acts suspicious and has lied to me several times." Eden paused to contemplate whether to ask her next question. The subject had been breached, so why not? "Do you mind if I ask what happened?"

Mrs. Emmet stared past Eden at the hospital. Eden berated herself, realizing she had upset her host. She brushed her hair from her face and returned her gaze to Eden. "Saturday night, after we left The Pizza Parlor, we came home. I took my nightly medicine. It helps me sleep, you see. I have fitful bouts of anxiety. Anyway, Roger left to go work at the hospital and I turned in. When I woke up the next morning he wasn't home, and there was no sign that he had been." For a moment she seemed as if she would cry, but she took a deep breath, glanced at the hospital, and continued. "I went to the hospital to see if he had worked all night."

"Did you see anything unusual in his lab?" Eden asked.

"No. I have to confess I don't go over there often, but everything looked as I had expected."

Eden turned toward the hospital. The empty parking lot shouted desertion while the trimmed shrubbery and recently painted building said 'ready for business.'

"What does the doctor do at the hospital?" Eden asked. "I thought it was closed."

"He's retired from practicing, but he does some research for a medical supply company in Wichita. I don't know much about the business, but it keeps him busy and the extra money is nice."

Eden took a step down and turned back toward Mrs. Emmet. "You mentioned this afternoon that you saw Sam Nelson outside on Saturday evening. When did that happen?"

"Shortly after Roger left; before I turned in. He walked by, drunk as usual."

Eden had been so engrossed in the conversation she hadn't noticed the blue sedan that parked in front of Mrs. Emmet's house. When Mrs. Emmet's attention shifted to a point behind Eden, she turned and saw a tall, older gentleman wave as he exited the car. His bald head was highlighted on each side with a gray strip. He was dressed much like the doctor had been the night before—trousers and a jacket—but in a more modern style.

"Hello, Gaylord."

"Hello, Stephanie."

Eden's body stiffened. Gaylord had looked vaguely familiar, but his voice was unmistakable. He was the one who had handed Lucas the envelope full of money.

"Eden, this is Gaylord Washburn. He's the mayor in Halstead. Gaylord, this is Eden Price."

Eden didn't even know who the mayor of Wichita was.

"It's very good to meet you Eden."

He shook her hand and she got the same chills throughout her body she had when she shook Jessica's cold, dry hand.

"I met Eden Saturday night. She works at The Pizza Parlor," Mrs. Emmet explained.

"Did you recently move to Halstead?" the mayor asked.

"I'm staying with my grandma and working for the summer."

The mayor smiled and nodded toward Mrs. Emmet. "Well, if there's ever anything you need, a friend of Stephanie's is a friend of mine."

"Thank you."

"And it's good to see that Stephanie's staying busy."

"Gaylord thinks I've gone off the deep end," she explained to Eden.

He shrugged. "I merely think she's overreacting. Roger has certainly gone away to do some research and will return soon enough." There wasn't a shred of doubt in his voice.

Eden shifted nervously. Could Dr. Emmet really be away on business? No, if that were the case then why pay Lucas to concoct some story? Should she say something?

"I told you he wouldn't have left without telling me," Mrs. Emmet scolded. "Eden believes me. She has a theory that Lucas Walls might have done something to Roger. You were at the hospital Saturday evening, weren't you, Gaylord?"

Now it was Mayor Washburn who shifted his weight, clearly uncomfortable with being put on the defensive.

"I was indeed. Ms. Barns and I were, um, discussing hospital business, if you must know."

"Gaylord is consulting with Jessica. They want to re-open the hospital." Mrs. Emmet addressed Eden before turning her attention back to Mayor Washburn.

"And were you two together the whole time?" Mrs. Emmet demanded.

"Except for the few minutes I stopped at The Pizza Parlor to pick up a pizza." He looked at Eden. "Do you remember? You were the one who handed it to me."

That's why he looked familiar! "I thought I recognized you from somewhere."

"Look. Roger had been talking about going to Dallas for research, and that's surely what he's done. Did you take your medicine Saturday evening?"

Eden fumed. The mayor was lying. "But—" She caught herself. It would be her word against his. And who would Mrs. Emmet believe? Certainly not Eden. And confronting him now would only upset her new friend. She shouldn't say anything yet.

Mrs. Emmet reacted to the mayor as if she hadn't heard Eden. "Of course I did! I take it every night."

"When Stephanie takes her medicine someone could take her house apart piece by piece and walk away with every square inch and she wouldn't wake up."

It was quite the exaggeration, but Mrs. Emmet didn't refute it.

"See? Her silence is proof," Mayor Washburn announced proudly.

"It's true," she admitted. "One time I slept for nine days."

"Really?" Eden asked, astonished.

"I think there were other factors at work. She was also running a fever and not feeling well," Mayor Washburn explained. His tone changed, sounding more sympathetic. "I'm sure Roger told you about his trip and you don't remember because you were drugged."

"Did he tell *you* where he was going?" Eden asked the mayor.

"Well, yes, he's talked for a while now about going to Dallas."

Apparently Mrs. Emmet had enough and went back on the offensive. "Eden thinks Lucas Walls could be involved. Did you see him around the hospital any time Saturday evening?"

He shook his head. "Is that the high school kid who does occasional errands for the doctor?"

Oh, good grief! Now he's pretending not to know Lucas? She had to consciously loosen her clenched jaw and fists.

"Yes," Mrs. Emmet said. "You know him?"

"I know *of* him, but I don't know him personally. No, I didn't see anyone around the hospital that evening."

"Well, it sure was nice to meet you," Eden said as she quickly trotted off. She had to get away from the mayor.

Chapter 7

On her walk home Eden saw Officer Dirks pull into the police station parking space and go inside, alone, so she followed him in.

The front lobby was new but modest. Photos of each Halstead police officer and volunteer hung on the front wall. It took Eden a moment to find Officer Dirk's picture, as it had been taken before he grew his moustache. Mickey's picture could have been taken that morning.

The only furniture included two chairs and a rack of brochures that included the neighborhood watch programs, bicycle safety, D.A.R.E. programs, and drunk driving statistics. The top ten Kansas most wanted list hung above the brochure rack. Eden pictured Lucas's mug on the list.

The door chimed when Eden entered, catching Officer Dirk's attention. He returned to the narrow counter and greeted her.

"What can I do for you this evening, Miss Price?"

She almost turned around without saying anything, but then thought of Lucas yelling at her in The Pizza Parlor and in the street. "I don't think Lucas acted alone."

"Is this about the body in his trunk you think you saw?" he asked patiently.

"I know what I saw."

His chest leaned into his arms on the counter. "And we checked it out. There was no evidence that Dr. Emmet, or anyone, had been in Lucas's car. I believe Officer Johnson explained that to you already."

"That's what I'm trying to say. Lucas and Officer Johnson are cousins. I think Mickey may be helping Lucas."

Officer Dirks took the news in stride. "That's quite an accusation. Do you have any evidence?"

She leaned with her back against the wall. "Well, no. But I know I saw a body in his trunk, and then Officer Johnson didn't see the body and he and Lucas were all buddy-buddy after that."

This brought loud laughter from the policeman. "I assure you, Mickey wouldn't be mixed up in anything illegal."

"But it's the only thing that makes sense."

"Mickey is the most by-the-book officer I've known. His first week on the job he wrote *me* a ticket for not using my turn signal. I think he'd give his own mom a ticket if he caught her jaywalking." He laughed again. "I guarantee he isn't aiding Lucas in anything sinister."

"But—"

"Besides, I was with Mickey when he searched Lucas's car. Trust me, Dr. Emmet was not there."

Crap, she did not see that coming!

"I also saw Mayor—"

Officer Dirks held up his hand. "Hold on, Miss Price. Before you go accusing anyone else, do you have any evidence?"

Eden hung her head. Why did she keep doing this to herself?

"In spite of what you see on TV, police don't work on empty theories and hunches. We follow the evidence."

She nodded, defeated.

"I'll tell you what, Miss Price. I'll check to see if anyone saw Lucas at the hospital last night. Will that make you happy?"

"Well, no, not exactly. But it's a start."

Eden exited the police station, stunned and confused. Mickey's involvement had been the most logical explanation for the lack of evidence in Lucas's trunk. But if Officer Dirks also searched the car, well, surely they couldn't *both* be involved, could they? Along with the mayor, whom she *knew* was involved with Dr. Emmet's disappearance? No, that seemed too absurd. But how could they not find any evidence? She knew what she saw. This seemed to be a conspiracy of epic proportions.

She needed proof. Anything to show Lucas was tied to the kidnapping.

Jessica wouldn't let her search the doctor's lab. The police weren't helping and didn't consider Lucas a suspect. She relented. The only thing she could do was get a good night's sleep and start fresh tomorrow.

A block from Mrs. Emmet's house, a teenage boy, probably a couple of years younger than her she guessed, rode through the intersection on his bike, a baseball bat sitting on his shoulder with a glove hanging from the handle. Eden tried to wave him down, but the boy shouted back at her, "I can't stop; I'm late for practice."

She reached the intersection and watched as the tardy player turned left where the road ended. Beyond stood a fence and light posts. A baseball field maybe?

An hour or two remained of sunlight, so Eden walked that direction. Soon she heard the clinging sound of bat meeting ball, and when she reached the end of the road, she saw that the field she had spotted sat empty. But, the one beside it was alive with teenage boys with baseball mitts.

A dozen or so spectators sat in bleachers behind home plate and another two dozen or so stood along the fence or sat in foldout chairs. One lady sat on a blanket with one little one coloring while another waved its stubby arms and legs, not yet old enough to crawl.

Eden crossed her arms comfortably on the top of the chain linked fence. Was she on the right field side of the field or the left field side? She never could remember which was which. She stood near first base.

The players—half in blue and half in white uniforms—huddled near home base for a minute then broke their huddle with a loud, "Go Dragons!"

The P.A. system squeaked, then an excited voice proclaimed, "Welcome to tonight's scrimmage featuring the State-bound Halstead Dragons baseball team."

The crowd cheered, then clapped enthusiastically as the starters on both sides were announced. A player wearing blue—one of the boys who had been with Lucas when she met him in the Pizza Parlor—threw the ball from a hill to the guy who wore all the gear. Catcher! The name finally popped into Eden's head.

Lucas and another player, in white and wearing helmets, swung bats (Lucas swung two at the same time) while exchanging words.

The catcher yelled, "Balls in!" and three balls that had been used to play catch went flying toward the dugout by first base. The players in the infield threw the ball to each other and then returned it to the pitcher. Eden knew this all had to do with their warm up ritual, but she didn't understand why.

"Hi Eden!" Ashley joined her leaning against the fence.

"Hi Ashley."

"It's so exciting, the team going to the State playoffs."

If you say so, Eden thought, but said. "They're pretty good?"

"Yeah, only lost three games all year."

"Play ball!"

Eden did a double take. With the padding underneath his shirt and the black cap sitting backwards on his head, she hadn't recognized him until she heard his voice. Officer Johnson, Mickey, placed the mask over his face and crouched behind the catcher.

"Go Dragons!" Ashley shouted.

"Which side are you rooting for?"

She shrugged. "Neither. It's just a practice game to get ready for the State tournament."

She seemed awfully enthused for a pretend game.

Lucas batted first and hit a hard ground ball to the other side of the field. The player picked up the ball and threw it to first base.

"Out!" Mickey hollered from halfway between first and home.

"How come he's out? They didn't tag him?"

"It's called a force play," Ashley patiently explained. "Since Lucas has to get to the base the defense only has to touch the bag while holding the ball to get the out. If Lucas had the option of going back to the previous base, then they would have to tag him."

The second batter hit the ball hard, but the left fielder, according to Ashley, made a nice, diving catch. The third batter hit a slow ground ball that the pitcher picked up and tossed easily to the first baseman for the out. They changed sides.

The white team warmed up similarly to the blue team, until Mickey finally yelled, "Batter up!"

The first batter swung and missed at three straight pitches. Eden hadn't watched a lot of baseball, but it seemed like Lucas really threw the ball hard. Harder than the first pitcher had thrown it, for sure. The next batter hit the fourth pitch high in the air and the first baseman caught it not far from Eden. The third batter struck out and the teams traded places again.

The next inning was similar to the first. No one reached base or scored. Same for the top of the third inning.

In the bottom of the inning, the first batter hit a ground ball to the second baseman, who threw the ball low and the first baseman couldn't catch it. "Safe!" Mickey announced.

"Error on the shortstop," the announcer informed.

Shortstop? "What's a shortstop?" Eden asked Ashley.

"That's the player between second and third base."

Eden had thought he was the second baseman. "Why do they call him a shortstop?"

Ashley pointed to the players. "Well, since they have four infielders and only three bases, I guess they needed a different name. I'm not sure where the name comes from."

The runner took a lead from first base. Lucas threw the ball to the first baseman, but the runner returned to the bag standing up. Ashley explained that the runner could get a lead and run to second if he wanted, but he had to avoid being tagged. Lucas, the pitcher, had to keep him from leaving too early so the catcher could have a chance to throw him out. The next time Lucas threw over, the runner had to dive to beat the throw.

"Time!" Mickey held both arms high in the air, one gripping his mask. He marched halfway to first base and yelled at the first baseman, "You have to stand in fair territory."

The player looked at his feet then back at Mickey and shrugged. Lucas joined Mickey, who now stood only a few feet from the first baseman. Mickey pointed toward his feet, speaking in a normal voice, but Eden could hear clearly.

"You can't be in foul territory. Both of your feet have to be in fair territory."

"I've never heard of that rule," the first baseman protested.

"Rule 4.03. 'When the ball is put in play at the start of, or during a game, all fielders other than the catcher shall be on fair territory.'"

"Huh? Are you serious?"

"I don't make the rules, I just enforce them." Mickey turned his back and returned to home plate. That was the end of the conversation.

"Is he serious?" he asked Lucas, once Mickey was far away not to hear.

Lucas laughed. "Dead serious. If he said it, I guarantee you it's in the rule book."

Lucas returned to the mound and the runner took a lead. The first baseman shook his head, set up to hold the runner, then looked down to make sure his feet were in fair territory. The ball went sailing past him. The runner stood on third base laughing by the time the right fielder (according to Ashley) had returned the ball to the pitcher. Lucas leaned forward with both hands on his knees, shaking his head in disgust.

"Is that a real rule?" Eden asked Ashley, apparently the resident baseball expert.

"I've never heard of it, but I also haven't read the rule book."

Lucas struck out that batter, but the next one hit a soft fly ball to right field, and the runner tagged and scored after the ball was caught. Ashley had to explain the sacrifice rule to Eden. Lucas and the white team got the next two batters out and they switched sides again.

Ashley turned her attention to Eden. "You said the other day that you don't believe in God?"

"That's right."

"Why not?"

Who talks about God? Isn't that what Bible studies are for? Eden really didn't have a good reason but with just a moment's thought came up with one. "I guess I've never had any use for God. Besides, if He wanted me to believe in Him, wouldn't He say something?"

"I think God's constantly trying to communicate with us."

Eden waited for more, but Ashley seemed to have turned her attention back to the game. Wasn't she going to try to convert Eden? Isn't that what Christians did? Or were supposed to do? What a strange girl. But nice.

They chatted off and on for the next couple of innings, mostly about the game with Ashley explaining more of the rules and why players did what they did.

The game was slow and relaxing, almost to the point of boring many times, which allowed her and Ashley to chat without much distraction.

Ashley called the game a pitcher's duel because the pitchers were doing really well and not many people got on base; in fact, the only run scored had been in the third inning.

After three innings, Lucas moved to center field and a new pitcher took his place. Ashley explained this was because Lucas was the best pitcher and the coaches didn't want Lucas to throw too many pitches so his arm would be fresh for the state tournament.

Neither team scored in the fourth inning, but in the top of the fifth, the white team scored two runs to take a 2-1 lead, with one final at bat for the blue team.

The lights above were now on and the sky neared the completion of nightfall. The warm air had dropped to a comfortable temperature.

The first batter for the blue team didn't hit the ball. In fact, he didn't even swing but Mickey told him to go to first base.

"Why does he get to be on base without hitting the ball?"

"That's called a walk," Ashley explained. "The pitcher has to throw strikes to give the batter a chance to hit the ball. If he doesn't, the player automatically gets on base."

The runner, the first since the earlier disaster for the first baseman, took a lead and quickly dove back, beating the throw from the pitcher. He took a lead again, the pitcher staring him down, pausing for a long time, Eden thought.

"Time!"

Much like earlier, Mickey walked toward first base and pointed at the first baseman's feet. "This is your last warning. You have to stay in fair territory."

The player's shoulders slumped and Eden imagined a look of anger on his face as he watched Mickey return to home plate. He looked at the placement of his carefully placed feet, glanced toward home plate, then stuck out his glove, waiting for a possible pickoff attempt. The pitcher threw to home and Mickey called out, "Strike!"

The first baseman had seemed to learn from his third inning blunder, and now merely glanced at his feet to make sure they were in the proper location. He again stretched out his glove as the runner took a lead. Eden found the whole scene suspenseful as her hands tightened around the top of the fence.

The pitcher threw toward home and the base runner took off toward second, but stumbled.

"Strike two!" Mickey hollered as the runner scrambled back toward first.

Ashley squealed and Eden jumped up and down and shouted, "Hurry!" Urging the runner to get back to first base before the catcher threw the ball, which he did, diving head first and stirring up dust that the wind blew just past the two girls. She surprised herself by shouting, and Eden realized she was rooting against Lucas's team.

"Safe!" Mickey yelled.

The runner called time and brushed himself off. He was filthy.

They repeated their routine. First baseman glanced at his feet, the runner took a lead, and the pitcher stared him down. This time, though, Eden noticed the first baseman shift his feet in anticipation of the throw that came almost immediately. The play was close but Eden clearly saw the player tag the runner before his hand found first base.

"Balk!"

Mickey removed his mask, marched part way toward first, and pointed for the runner to go to second base.

The pitcher threw up his hands in frustration. "What did I do?"

"It wasn't you." Mickey pointed toward first base. "He was in foul territory when you threw him the ball. That's a violation of rule 4.03, and the result is that the player is awarded one base."

"That's crap, man!" the first baseman protested.

Mickey pointed a finger and narrowed the gap considerably. "You can look it up yourself after the game, but in the meantime, one more word and I'll have to toss you out."

The players face reddened and he clenched his jaw tight, but he kept his mouth shut and kicked first base in frustration after Mickey had turned to walk back to home plate.

Apparently the pitcher was rattled too. The next pitch he threw so high that the catcher couldn't jump high enough to grab it. The runner jogged easily to third base. He threw three more straight balls and now runners were on first and third with no outs and a one-run game.

"This is exciting!" Ashley yelled at Eden.

The crowd, which had been mostly quiet throughout, was cheering loudly with each pitch.

After another ball to the next batter, the pitcher threw a strike and the runner at first base took off for second. The catcher pumped his arm like he threw the ball but didn't, then whirled and threw the ball to third base. The runner just made it back in time.

The catcher called time out and all of the infield players huddled in front of the pitcher's mound.

"The coaches let the players make decisions during the scrimmages," Ashley explained to Eden. "They like the players to develop leadership and critical thinking skills."

When everyone returned to their positions, the catcher remained standing and held his arm straight out. It looked really strange.

"What is he doing now?" Eden asked

"They're going to intentionally walk the batter."

Give him a free base? "Why would they do that?"

Ashley pointed as she explained. "Since they only have a one-run lead and this is the last inning, the batter doesn't matter. If the player at third scores, then the game is tied and if the player on second scores, then the game is over. So, they put this batter on first base and that way they only have to tag home plate and not the runner, making it easier to keep him from scoring."

Eden nodded like she understood. She only kind of did.

The pitcher threw the ball and the catcher had to jump sideways to catch it. The batter took his stance, the catcher stuck out his arm, then stepped sideways to catch the pitch. The pitcher threw the ball.

"Balk!"

The pitcher stormed toward home plate and demanded, "What are you talking about?"

The first baseman arrived right after him. Eden glanced in the dugout and the coaches smiled, enjoying the scenario.

"The catcher is not allowed to leave his position behind home plate until the ball is pitched. He clearly stepped to the side before you threw the ball, putting him in foul territory and breaking rule 4.03a. The result of the play is a balk, and each of the base runners advances one base. I can quote the rule for you if you like, but it's rather long."

Eden watched Lucas in center field as he squatted on one knee and shook his head in disbelief.

The pitcher and catcher argued for another minute or two, but it was in vain. The runner on third base scored to tie the game 1-1 and the other base runner advanced to third.

The white team successfully intentionally walked the next two batters to load the bases, still with no outs. The next batter struck out swinging.

The crowd had grown to over fifty or more since the start, and everyone was on their feet, clapping and cheering with each pitch.

"Ball one. Strike one. Ball two. Strike two." Anticipation grew with each pitch. Eden stood on her tiptoes as if that helped her be significantly closer to the action.

The next pitch the batter lifted high in the air. The runner on third returned to the bag and Eden tried to get a beat on the ball.

Lucas waved his hands and lightly jogged forward until the ball had nearly arrived. Then he sped up, and in one fluid motion caught the ball, hopped, and grunted loudly as he threw the ball toward home plate.

The runner plowed down the line, on a direct collision course with the catcher standing at home plate. The ball bounced somewhere between the pitcher's mound and home plate and landed perfectly in the catcher's glove, who swooped down to place a tag.

Mickey's arms flew sideways. "Safe!"

The blue team celebrated and for several moments many in the crowd cheered.

"Wow, that was exciting!" Eden shouted. She could see why people enjoyed the game.

"And that was just a practice game," Ashley reminded her. "Wait until State!"

The moon had replaced the sun and brought a slight chill in the air as Eden left the practice game with Ashley. They traveled two blocks together before Ashley turned toward her house.

As Eden passed the intersection near the police station, she heard yelling come from the direction of the hospital, so instead of heading home, she decided to check out the ruckus.

A block later she could clearly hear Sam's ranting as he stood swaying in front of the Emmet residence. "You tell that no-good, yellow-bellied, chicken to come out of his hiding and face me like a man. He owes me an apology and I reckon to stay here until I gets one."

Dr. and Mrs. Emmet's house remained completely dark. Eden chuckled. Mrs. Emmet had probably taken her medicine and retired for the evening. From what she and Mayor Washburn had said, Mrs. Emmet would stay asleep, even if Sam yelled all night. She turned to go home but then had an idea. She took off running toward Sam's house. Okay, running had been a bad idea. After half a block she stopped and doubled over. Once she'd caught her breath, she kept it to a brisk walk.

Still, she arrived at his house breathless. As she approached Sam's front door, she looked around the neighborhood. She didn't see anyone, so she walked straight up to the door and turned the knob. Jackpot. When the door opened, she marched straight in like she belonged.

Eden quickly found Sam's journal and fled the house.

Chapter 8

Eden was anxious to read Sam's journal, but her grandmother sat at the card table working on her puzzle listening to some soft jazz. Eden wouldn't have to play Yahtzee tonight but she might have to stare at the eight hundred or so pieces still to be placed in Maimeo's puzzle of a litter of puppies.

She tried to give Maimeo a quick hello and disappear back to her bedroom, but her grandmother asked her to sit and tell about her day; even offered to make popcorn in exchange for Eden's company. Sam's journal, hiding underneath the living room couch, would have to wait.

Eden studied the box cover for a moment. Six different colored puppies crawling on top of one another inside a straw basket.

Maimeo had the edge done and was at work on the grass underneath the basket. She decided to look for basket pieces.

"How was your visit with Mrs. Emmet?"

"It was good. She's really nice. Did you know they liked Halstead so much that Dr. Emmet retired instead of moving away?"

"Yes, Stephanie did tell me that."

Eden bounced excitedly because she found two pieces that went together. Sometimes her helping Maimeo on a puzzle wasn't very productive.

"We talked for like an hour and a half. Then I saw a boy rushing to the baseball field so I followed and watched a scrimmage of the high school baseball team. They're really good. At least that's what Ashley says."

Maimeo smiled. "You couldn't tell if they were good?"

"They throw the ball hard and stuff, but I don't watch baseball so I don't know."

They worked for several minutes with just the relaxing instrumental music for sound. Maimeo had a small corner of the puzzle finished and Eden had only found three pieces that connected.

"I don't remember you working puzzles when I was younger. Is this a new hobby?" Eden tossed a handful of popcorn into her mouth.

Maimeo paused and looked up, her eyes distant as if in memory. "After your grandpa passed away a few years ago I was so, so lonely. I sunk into a deep depression. For months I barely left the house, sometimes stayed in bed all day. I think your mom got tired of my attitude and taking care of me because she yelled that I could at least one time pretend to be normal for you and her.

She said she couldn't take it anymore. I had been so focused on my sorrow that I didn't realize I was hurting my two favorite people. So, the next day I made myself go shopping.

"While out, I saw an old puzzle in a thrift store exactly like one I helped my grandma with nearly fifty years earlier. As soon as I dumped the pieces on my dining room table I felt like a young girl and I swear I could feel Grandma's presence. For the first time in weeks I felt calm and not so lonely.

"I finished the puzzle in less than a week, glued it together, and it was the first thing I hung up when I moved to Halstead."

Eden nodded toward the Golden Gate Bridge puzzle hanging behind Maimeo. "Is that the puzzle?"

Her grandmother looked fondly at the old puzzle and smiled as she continued. "I got to the end and several pieces were missing, but I didn't care. I realized that puzzle was just like me. So many things in my life had created holes in me, like those missing pieces did to the puzzle.

Yet, I can't put into words how valuable that puzzle is to me. So if an old, incomplete and discarded puzzle can wield so much value, an old fogy like me must be worth more than sitting around the house day after day feeling sorry for herself.

"I decided I wanted a different life; one full of friends and laughter and love. I researched small towns around

Wichita, moved to Halstead, and started going to church and volunteering. I even started a book club so that I could meet people and make friends."

Maimeo continued to look at the puzzle on the wall so Eden drew her focus back to the basket. When her grandmother turned around, Eden asked, "Do you still think of your grandma when you work on puzzles?"

"Mm, hmm. Every time."

Eden wondered if one day fifty years from now she would think back to this day and how much her grandmother meant to her. She felt tears welling up so she stood to get herself a glass of water.

They worked for another twenty minutes or so, but Maimeo seemed to be in a distant time, probably decades in the past. Eden managed to make progress on the basket's handle before Maimeo excused herself to go to bed.

Eden changed into her comfortable long t-shirt that hung to her knees, grabbed another bowl of popcorn, and curled up on the loveseat in her grandmother's back room with Sam's journal.

Hopeful to find evidence connecting Lucas to Dr. Emmet and Mayor Washburn—and a morbid curiosity to read more of Sam's musings—she shoved a handful of popcorn in her mouth and opened the book.

At first she enjoyed his stories, until the deaths continued to get more and more graphic. She skipped ahead. Sam Nelson was quite the stalker. He had watched Dr.

Emmet closely this last year, even breaking into his house and the hospital to snoop around. Then she stumbled on the entry from March 14, 2021.

Dr. Emmet and Mayor Washburn took the doctor's wife into the hospital last night and she hasn't come out. The lights in the lab flashed blue and the lights around the area went off for several minutes, it seemed.

March 15, 2021. The doctor and his wife are still in the hospital. The mayor comes and goes.

March 16, 2021. I watched the hospital all day and still the doctor and his wife have not left. I've snuck into the hospital three days in a row but I can't get into the lab upstairs where the doctor does his experiments. The doctor hasn't left there for four days now. I think he must be doing some kind of experiment on his wife. Probably on her brain, from the looks of the machine he's built.

March 22, 2021. It's been nine days since Dr. Emmet and Mayor Washburn took Mrs. Emmet into the hospital. At around one this morning, I saw them carry her back to the doctor's house.

March 23, 2021. I pounded on the doctor's door today pretending to be drunk. I haven't had a drink in over a week. Mrs. Emmet opened the door and told me to go away.

She looked fine, and didn't even have her head bandaged. There was no visible sign she had undergone a medical procedure. What could she have been doing over at the hospital for nine days?

April 30, 2021. My drinking is getting worse. I blacked out for several days. I'm not even sure how many days, or how I survived. I'm going to quit.
May 8, 2021. The mayor took an ostrich into the hospital tonight. After he and the doctor left, I snuck into the hospital but couldn't find the ostrich anywhere. And like with all the other animals, I didn't see where it had been dissected. It's like it disappeared.

Oh, here's the date the doctor disappeared! Eden bounced up and down excitedly.

May 13, 2021. I saw the Wall's kid talking to Mayor Washburn. I saw the mayor leave and come back with a pizza. The ordinary weird light show went on up on the fourth story where the doctor's lab is. It was well after midnight at that point. I don't remember seeing the doctor leave. I don't remember how or when I got home.

Eden closed her eyes and tried to process all of the information.

Mrs. Emmet told her she went to bed and slept all night. The mayor said he was with Jessica all evening.

Then there was Lucas. He had said he didn't go to the hospital that night. He had lied to Eden—again.

No surprise.

Sam could be fabricating the story, but why would he lie in his journal? Maybe he wrote while drinking and got confused. But so much of his journal contained specific information that would be hard to discount.

She trusted the words of the town drunk over a boy her own age. It was sad, but true. She tried to put the pieces together but nothing fit. Tiredness overtook her and she drifted off.

Eden woke to an overwhelming fog of alcohol to find Sam's eyes inches from hers. He slapped his hand over her mouth before she could scream. His bloodshot eyes were full of rage. He looked deranged and Eden didn't think the devil himself could be any scarier. Every horrible odor coming from his body combined to create the atomic bomb of smell. Eden's eyes began to water. She gagged and thought she was going to throw up.

Sam smirked, his smile full of yellow teeth and gaping holes. He licked his lips like he might eat her. Without taking his eyes off of hers, he reached out with his free hand.

It found her shoulder. With only the thin t-shirt between his hand and her skin, Eden wished she had on more than just panties underneath the shirt. She closed her eyes as tight as she could and prayed this was a dream.

He slid his hand down her arm and stopped when it found her hand. "There it is," he growled. He snatched his journal and held it up close to her face. "Don't ever touch my journal again. Ever." He giggled sinisterly. "Do you understand?" He nodded his head and she mirrored him.

"Don't ever tell anyone I was here. Understand?" He nodded his head again and she did likewise. "When I remove my hand don't scream. Understand?" A third time he nodded his head and she readily agreed.

"You read my stories in here?"

Eden's ears burned with shame. She nodded again.

"So you know what I'm capable of if you break one of the rules we just agreed on. Right?"

She quickly nodded.

"I'd hate for anything to happen to this pretty face of yours." He giggled again. "Or to your grandma."

She shook her head rapidly. He drew his face close to hers. The grip of his hand on her mouth loosened and she thought he was going to kiss her. Instead, he took a deep sniff of her hair and quietly left through the back door.

Eden wanted to cry or scream, but she couldn't move. For half an hour she sat paralyzed. Finally, her breathing returned to normal and her fear subsided. She ran to the bathroom, ripped off her clothes, and jumped in the shower. She scrubbed her skin raw, then sank into a sitting position and sobbed.

Chapter 9

*E*arly the next morning Eden sat on the edge of her bed in a white robe. She nodded off, then blinked her eyes several times and took a deep breath.

Thinking it would take more than Mountain Dew or coffee to energize herself, she did something drastic, jumping jacks. She made it to six—why did she count them anyway—and abruptly stopped when she noticed the crumpled up twenty-dollar bill. Mrs. Emmet had told her to spend it, but before that the doctor had told her to read it, "when the time was right". That whole exchange had seemed odd.

She unfolded the bill and rubbed it against the edge of the dresser several times to smooth it out. Across the top of Andrew Jackson's thick, wavy hair was written the word "she." Across his large forehead was the word "knows."

"She knows?" Eden said to herself. "Who is she and what does she know?"

There were four letters circled on the front of the bill. The I-T-E in *United* and the M in *America*. "She knows item. Hmm."

There were more letters circled on the back. The letter H was circled in the word *The*, N, I, and E were circled in *United*, and the M, C, and A were circled in *America*. "Let's see, H-N-I-E-M-C-A. That doesn't spell anything."

Eden took pen and paper from her desk and wrote down the letters. "What if I rearrange the letters..." She studied the letters for a minute or two then wrote something down. "Item machine?"

Dr. Emmet had told her to read it when the time was right. What if he hadn't misspoken as his wife had presumed? Could Dr. Emmet have been trying to give her a message? Maybe he knew he was in trouble and wanted Eden to read the note after he disappeared? No, how could he have known? In *case* he disappeared? Surely it was just a big coincidence.

Eden dressed, quickly brushed her hair, put the $20 bill in her jeans pocket and made a cup of Green Mountain Hazelnut coffee in the Keurig. She sat on her grandma's front porch, wondering if Dr. Emmet was trying to tell her something.

As he left his house, Lucas covered his yawn with a brown baseball glove. He leapt over the three porch steps before settling into a casual pace toward his car, which had the top up. He looked at Eden and quickened his pace.

"What? No snide remark or degrading insult this morning?" Eden hollered.

He ignored her. Eden started after him. What was she doing? She wasn't normally confrontational, but when it came to Lucas, something inside of her insisted he needed to be the exception. When he saw her on the attack, he broke into a speed walk. At the car he fumbled in the pocket of his khaki shorts, and then clumsily dropped the keys on the ground.

This flustered side of Lucas tickled Eden. She easily reached him before he got his car door unlocked.

"I know you lied to me about being at the hospital Friday night. I know you were there with Mayor Washburn. I know you met with the mayor yesterday and that he gave you some money. I know you're involved with Dr. Emmet's disappearance, I just don't know how." She paused for dramatic effect. "Yet."

Lucas's mouth gaped and he dropped his keys again. Eden felt giddy.

It was way too late, but he tried to be nonchalant. "So what? The doctor owed me some money. Mayor Washburn agreed to pay it since he isn't around."

"No, the mayor gave you money to keep quiet about the doctor."

He opened his mouth as if to say something, then spun back to his car.

"What's going on with you today?"

"What do you mean?"

"No insults. You ignored me instead of making me feel worthless. I'm challenging you with questions and you aren't angry. You aren't your usual, despicable self."

"Look, I just want you to leave me alone. I need to focus on preparing for the State tournament and don't want any more distractions. I figured if I left you alone you could leave me alone and we could each pretend the other doesn't exist."

He was worried; she must be getting close. "Two days ago I would have taken you up on that offer, but now I know you're involved with Dr. Emmet's disappearance and I can't let that go. I am going to figure out what you've done."

"Ahh!" Lucas screamed in frustration. "You're like an annoying fly, buzzing around my head and no matter how much I swat and how hard I try to kill you, you keep flying around and bothering me until I have to get out of bed and go sleep on the couch because you won't leave me alone, but you follow me out to the couch and keep landing on my nose and my eyelids then crawl up my neck until I get goose bumps and I don't get any sleep all night and fail my English test the next day because you wouldn't leave me alone!"

Eden smiled. "I'm flattered."

"Flattered?"

"I didn't realize you thought about me that much."

Lucas screamed and kicked his tire. "Just leave me alone!"

She sipped her coffee and contemplated. "Answer a question for me and I won't bother you anymore."

"What's your—"

"Today."

"Today what?"

"I won't bother you any more today. At least I'll try not to. I promise." She smiled innocently.

Lucas sighed. "What's your question?"

"What does the doctor do in the hospital?"

Lucas shrugged. "He does some work for the mayor's medical company in Wichita. I think he develops drugs and medical equipment."

"What kind of equipment?"

Lucas shook his head. "I don't know."

"You have to know something," she insisted. "You run errands and do things for him. I'm sure you've been in there plenty of times. Take your best guess at what he's up to."

Lucas had a frightened look on his face. "I went inside the hospital one time. Never again."

"Why not?" Eden asked and took another drink of her coffee.

"It's haunted."

Eden spewed coffee on his Mustang. She tried to wipe the burn from her nose as she laughed. She noticed that Lucas was wide-eyed and didn't seem to even notice she had just spit coffee on his precious car. "You... you're serious? Haunted? Like ghosts?"

"Yes, ghosts." Lucas frowned. "I snuck into the hospital one night after the doctor and Mayor Washburn had left. I wanted to know what was going on in there, like you do. Well, there were all kinds of weird noises. I heard footsteps but there wasn't anyone else around."

"Maybe that was just your mind playing tricks on you," Eden offered.

"Maybe. Maybe not. But what happened next there is no explanation for." Lucas looked around like the enemy might be listening in on a national security discussion. "I went to the top floor. That's where Dr. Emmet has his lab. There's a strange-looking machine in there. I don't know what it does, but it's ground-breaking, at least from what I've gathered from Dr. Emmet and Mayor Washburn." *That would explain the machine reference on the twenty-dollar bill.*

"I searched the lab and the adjacent room, then left to search the rest of the floor. I heard, I heard...*Baaa.*" Lucas's impression of a goat was impressive. Eden wanted to laugh, but resisted since he was intensely serious.

"I went back to the lab and there was a goat. I swear it hadn't been there a minute before. That room had been empty and that door was the *only* way in or out. Now how does a goat appear out of nowhere? There were ghosts or demons or something messing with me."

The earnest focus in his eyes convinced Eden that he believed every word he said. "So you believe in ghosts and phantoms and things like that?"

"Of course. There's too many weird things that happen that can only be explained by the supernatural."

She leaned against his car. He looked at her disapprovingly but didn't say anything. She decided not to push it and stepped away. "There's always an explanation."

"Not always," Lucas argued.

"We can't always see what the explanation is," Eden said, "but there's always a scientific explanation."

"So you don't believe in ghosts?"

"No. I have to be able to see how something exists before I believe in it."

He moved his cap, wiped his forehead with his arm. "You don't believe in anything you can't see?" Lucas asked.

She took another drink. "Not exactly. I said I have to see how it *could* exist."

"What do you mean?"

"For instance, I believe there is probably extraterrestrial life on another planet. I believe time travel is possible. I believe mind-reading may be possible."

"You believe in aliens and time travel but not ghosts?" Lucas asked, stunned.

"I think there's evidence that life can exist on another planet and that extraterrestrial life may have already visited Earth. And even Stephen Hawking believes time travel is a possibility."

"Yeah, well, there's plenty of evidence that ghosts exist," Lucas countered, pointing his cap at her. "Did you see Paranormal Activity? Or Paranormal Activity two, three, or four?"

Eden rolled her eyes. "I think we're going to have to agree to disagree on ghosts."

"You go into the hospital some night and walk around and see if you still don't believe in ghosts when you're done," Lucas challenged.

"I plan to check out the hospital but I won't be looking for ghosts."

Chapter 10

Eden hadn't taken two steps through the back door at work before Ashley was already talking a mile a minute.

"Hi Eden. I looked into Officer Johnson. He has a solid reputation, although there is one thing. I have an older brother his age that went to school with Mickey. He said in fifth grade he got in trouble for putting a garter snake in a girl's backpack. But sorry, that's the worst I could come up with. My brother said Mickey was a good student and never caused any problems in school. I guess that isn't much help."

Eden clocked in. "Well, it's not the information I was hoping for, but it always helps to know the truth."

"Did you find out any more? Have you done any more investigating?" Ashley asked with an eager glint in her eye.

Had she ever learned a lot! But Eden hesitated to share too much, so she focused on Lucas. "Lucas acted really strange this morning. Instead of being angry and confrontational, he wanted us to ignore each other."

"Wow! What brought that on?" Ashley asked.

Eden washed and dried her hands. "I don't know."

"What did you tell him? Did you agree to leave each other alone? Will that affect your case?"

"I can leave him alone, alright. I'm still determined to know what he's involved with. He seemed genuine, but my guess is he just wants me to stay out of his business. I think he's afraid I'll figure out what he did and tell the police—which is exactly what I intend to do. I must be getting close."

Eden noticed she was rubbing her hands together and quickly dropped them, but not before Ashley had also noticed.

"Do you think you can still be objective? I mean, what if he didn't have anything to do with Dr. Emmet disappearing?"

"I'll let the facts lead me," Eden said, nodding firmly. "And they're leading right to Lucas. I just need to find more facts."

Ashley bit her fist. "It's just that vengeance can cloud a person's judgment."

"This isn't about vengeance," Eden assured her. "It's about justice. Lucas is guilty and I'm the only one who sees it."

Eden followed Ashley to the counter. For the next two hours she answered the phone and helped bus tables.

Eden bored of the tasks so as the lunch crowd slowed and the phone remained silent, she asked Ashley if she could run the register.

"There's no sense in me showing you how to use it. We're getting a new one delivered this afternoon."

"I've run one similar to this. I don't think I need much guidance."

Ashley stepped back. "It's all yours, then."

Eden helped several customers with little input from Ashley. During the next lull, Eden remembered what she'd wanted to tell Ashley.

"Lucas believes there are ghosts in the hospital."

"What?"

Eden quickly told her what Lucas had said about the goat in the hospital lab. "The only thing I can't figure out is what it could have really been. I don't believe in ghosts."

Ashley placed her hand on Eden's arm and said excitedly, "I don't either. There's no scientific evidence."

"I know, right?"

The phone rang and Eden answered. She wrote down the order and handed it to Ashley who delivered it to the kitchen staff to fill.

When Ashley returned, she continued. "You know, sometimes when we believe in something, our minds are powerful enough to convince us it's real."

Eden nodded. "I know that's true, but I also read in Sam's journal that he's seen the mayor take animals into the hospital." She quickly told Ashley about her conversation with Sam, leaving out the part where she stole his journal and he came into Maimeo's house and took it back.

"So what did Lucas do when he saw the goat he thought was put there by a ghost?" Ashley asked.

"He ran." Eden laughed.

Ashley shook her head. "I mean, teleporting would be a more scientific explanation. I don't think we're anywhere near having that technology, but at least it's logical. Or maybe the goat is a time traveler from a thousand years ago. Or maybe it was camouflaged somehow."

Eden agreed. "Any of those make more sense than a ghost."

Behind Eden the door dinged so she turned around to greet the customer. Standing in front of the counter with a scowl on her face was Jessica, the scary owner of the hospital.

Eden swallowed hard and forced a smile. "Welcome to The Pizza Parlor. How may I help you?"

"A BLT with a fruit cup and a large soda to go."

Eden's hand shook as she wrote the order on the ticket. When she tried to enter the order in the cash register, instead of ringing up a BLT she hit the key for the salad bar. She asked Ashley to help her fix it, but then hit coffee instead of soda. Her breathing grew rapid and she could feel her ears burn. She finally got the order entered correctly, after what had to have been two minutes of awkward silence and pushing buttons. "That will be $7.36."

Ashley handed the ticket to the kitchen as Eden took twenty dollars from Jessica, opened the drawer, and fumbled with the bills. All she could think about was how much she had screwed up and couldn't concentrate on how much change she owed Jessica. Normally doing the math in her head wouldn't have been a problem, but she was rattled. Finally, she intentionally dropped a few pennies. As she bent down to pick them up she snuck the order ticket and pen with her. She quickly did the math on the back of the receipt booklet then managed to give Jessica the correct change.

"It will be about five minutes," Ashley announced as she returned from the kitchen. "We'll bring it out to you when it's ready."

Ten minutes later when Eden carried the sack with Jessica's lunch inside and handed it to her, Jessica jabbed, "I'm not sure who was slower, you or the kitchen."

She left before Eden had a chance to respond.

Chapter 11

Ashamed of her cowardice, Eden decided to try again to explore the hospital. Surely she could find a way into the lab without getting caught. She knew somehow that Dr. Emmet's lab was key to his disappearance, so after her lunch shift ended she headed to the hospital.

She tried every door and window, but soon her hopes of finding a different entrance into the hospital were dashed. She had to resort to using the front door.

She entered the lobby and started down the dark hallway when she heard Mayor Washburn's voice coming from Jessica's office. Eden circled around to the opposite side and crept close enough to eavesdrop.

"Why are you so uptight?" Jessica asked sympathetically—a much different tone than Eden had experienced.

"I can't relax." A chair scooted and steps shuffled back and forth. "Next week is *the* week. We're supposed to get a big payday, but all the attention we're getting with Roger gone could sabotage the deal."

"So you know where he is?"

There was a long pause and the steps quit. "Yes."

Jessica gasped. "Please tell me you don't have anything to do with it."

The mayor chuckled, then spat with disdain, "What he's doing is threatening to cost me billions of dollars."

Eden slapped a hand over her mouth so she wouldn't give herself away. Billions? How could that be right?

"You know what happened to him?"

"Of course I do."

"Is he okay?" Jessica asked apprehensively.

"I don't know. It's that machine."

Jessica gasped again. "Does anyone else know?"

Eden knew that machine was key to all of this, and the mayor had confirmed it.

"No! But I don't know how long I can keep it that way. Mrs. Emmet nearly messed this whole thing up. No one would even know he was missing if she hadn't gone hysterical and run to the police."

Eden wished she could see them, but didn't dare get any closer. Should she be recording them? Surely her phone had a recording ability, but that might take time. What if someone called her or texted? She frantically pulled the phone from her back pocket and quieted the volume.

"What are you going to do?" True concern filled Jessica's voice.

"Deflect. The police had a tip that Lucas Walls might have been involved. Right now they're chasing that lead. It will buy some time, but I don't know how much."

"Lucas Walls? Isn't that the kid who makes the deliveries for Roger?"

"Yes. I bribed him to keep quiet about our experiments and to accept the blame for Dr. Emmet disappearing. I just hope it'll give me enough time."

"Does he know what you're really doing?" Jessica asked.

So Lucas didn't know anything about Dr. Emmet's disappearance? No, that couldn't be because Eden had seen the body. Her legs tired so she squatted to one knee.

The mayor laughed. "He has no idea what we're doing upstairs. In fact, I have to go outside when he makes deliveries. He won't step into the hospital; he's scared of ghosts. But if the kid said anything about the errands he runs for Roger, then the police might begin to ask questions that could ruin years of planning and labor."

"Do you think Lucas will be able to handle the heat?"

"For what I'm paying him, he'd better."

"There's something I need to tell you."

The shuffling stopped.

The quiet lasted so long, Eden held her breath; afraid to make any noise. Jessica continued and Eden slowly exhaled. "The afternoon before Roger disappeared, he confronted me; said he knew that I knew about the machine and what it could do."

Eden startled from what sounded like a fist slamming down on Jessica's desk.

Mayor Washburn exploded. "How could he have known you knew?"

"I don't know!" Jessica shot back.

The mayor let out a deep sigh. "What did you tell him?"

"Nothing. I denied it all, but he knew. He had no doubt. At least now he's out of the way."

Eden switched knees. She wanted to sit but feared she might have to run.

The mayor's shuffling feet resumed. "I have the city council meeting tonight. What if there are a lot of reporters, or people asking questions about Roger? What am I supposed to tell them?"

"Tell them you can't comment about an ongoing investigation," Jessica suggested. "Or better yet, tell them you heard from Dr. Emmet and he's traveling. It doesn't matter, does it? You just need to stall."

"I have a couple of things I need to do upstairs before the meeting tonight," Mayor Washburn said.

Drats! There went Eden's chance to look around the doctor's lab.

"Will you come back tonight?" Jessica asked in a voice suddenly sultry.

Eden gagged.

"Yeah, I'll be here like always," he said unenthusiastically.

Eden hurried down the hall and hid behind the front counter of the lobby. Once Mayor Washburn left Jessica's office and was out of sight, she left the hospital and ran to the police station.

Chapter 12

E den burst into the police station completely out of breath. Officer Dirks smiled. "Miss Price, what a pleasant surprise! I owe you a bit of an apology. It looks like you were partially right about Lucas Walls. We have a witness that saw him with Dr. Emmet shortly before he disappeared. We plan to bring Lucas in for questioning."

"No, you've got it all wrong!" Eden realized she was shouting way too loudly. "Lucas didn't have anything to do with Dr. Emmet's disappearance."

Officer Dirks removed his glasses and rubbed his eyes. "What? Two days ago you thought he was responsible. Now that we are looking into it, you're saying he didn't do it?"

"That's right." Eden's speech quickened. "Mayor Washburn wants you to think it was Lucas because *he's* done something with Dr. Emmet. I'm not sure what yet."

"Slow down a minute, Miss Price." She thought he was intentionally talking slower. "You're now saying that our mayor kidnapped Dr. Emmet?"

She intertwined her hands behind her head and paced. "I don't know if they took him, but they know what's going on."

"They?"

"Mayor Washburn and Jessica Barns. Dr. Emmet may not have even been taken; I don't know."

"You think Dr. Emmet may have left town and didn't tell anyone he was leaving?"

"Yes. Maybe. I don't know!" Eden knew she wasn't making sense, but she couldn't seem to communicate clearly. She stopped and faced the police chief, took a deep breath and slowed down. "I don't know yet what happened to Dr. Emmet, but I made a mistake in accusing Lucas. He wasn't involved. At least not directly."

"And how do you know Lucas wasn't involved?" Officer Dirks inquired.

"I overheard Mayor Washburn tell Jessica Barns that he was going to let him take the blame for Dr. Emmet's disappearance."

"You do realize that all you're giving me is hearsay and you are in danger of spreading rumors about two of Halstead's most respected citizens."

He was right. Eden didn't have any evidence. What had she been thinking, barging into the police station? She should have recorded the conversation! Then it hit her! She reached into her front pocket and pulled out the twenty-dollar bill Dr. Emmet had given her and handed it to Officer Dirks.

"What's this?"

"Dr. Emmet gave it to me a few hours before he disappeared."

"So?"

"So, he told me to read it when the time was right. I didn't know what he was talking about at the time. But then he disappeared, so it makes more sense."

Officer Dirks waved the bill in the air. "Help it make sense to me."

She took the bill from him and laid it flat, pointing as she spoke. "Dr. Emmet wrote on Andrew Jackson's head 'she knows.' Then he circled four letters on the front, I-T-E-M. He was trying to tell me that she knows something about an item."

"What item?" Officer Dirks asked.

She turned the bill over and showed him the back.

"What does H-N-I-E-M-C-A mean? That doesn't spell anything."

"No. But if you rearrange them they spell machine."

He looked at her, befuddled. "Machine?"

"It makes sense," Eden said excitedly, pointing in the direction she thought the hospital laid. "Dr. Emmet has been working on a machine and Mayor Washburn said the doctor disappearing could cost him billions of dollars. Maybe he built something they can sell."

Officer Dirks rubbed his eyes and forehead. "Billions? I think you misheard something."

"I know what I heard." Though it did sound outlandish.

"Still, what does it mean that she knows? And what about the word *item*?"

Eden had to admit she didn't know.

"Look, you've got an interesting story here, but that's all it is. The writing on this bill could have been written by anyone, and the rest is hearsay." He paused. "Are you saying now that Lucas didn't have something in his trunk?"

"Yes. I mean no. I did see something, someone, move in his trunk." She paused. "Do you believe me now?"

Officer Dirks shifted, nervously. "Well, we didn't find any evidence to support your claim."

"But now you think Lucas was involved?"

"We are investigating all leads," he answered diplomatically. "Miss Price, why don't you relax and enjoy your summer and let the police do their job?"

Eden left the police station deflated. She was sure that whatever the doctor and mayor were doing was much bigger than Officer Dirks believed. At least with them looking into Lucas, they might find their way to the truth. She had her doubts, though, since they couldn't even find evidence of who had been in Lucas' trunk. She had been the one to persuade the police to pursue Lucas for something he didn't do. He was willing to take the blame, so let him.

Officer Dirks was right; it was time for her to bow out.

Chapter 13

*E*den was relegated to kitchen duty while Ashley worked the front. Even with a small dinner crowd, Ashley struggled to keep up using the new cash register. Eden helped bus tables, then volunteered when Toby asked who wanted to leave early. She clocked out, but before she could sneak out the back door, Ashley called her over.

"Sorry you didn't get to work the front. The owner tends to go overboard on his purchases. The cash register is a lot nicer and more complex than we need. I'll get it figured out soon and get you trained on it."

Eden waved her off. "No problem. It was a slow day anyway."

"How is the case going?"

"I'm off it now."

Ashley covered her mouth, though not quite as dramatically as before. "Why? What happened?"

"I figured out that Lucas didn't do anything to Dr. Emmet." She explained how she'd overheard Lucas and

Mayor Washburn speaking and then Mayor Washburn and Jessica. "I know Lucas didn't do it even though he's willing to take the fall for it. Officer Dirks is checking into Lucas, so it's probably a matter of time before he gets blamed."

Ashley, ever the dramatic artist, stood with her mouth wide open and her hands on her hips. "You can't let him get into trouble for something he didn't do."

"Now you sound like Maimeo. What's the big deal? He's up to something, I just don't know what. Besides, after what he did to me it serves him right to get into trouble." Eden refused to have sympathy for him.

"But it's not right," Ashley insisted.

"It's karma," Eden countered.

"It's not right."

Eden shrugged. "I don't see the harm. Eventually they'll see Lucas didn't take the doctor and let him go. Besides, he had something in his trunk so he's not completely innocent."

Eden started to leave but Ashley grabbed her arm with surprising force.

"Eden, listen to me." Ashley did not let go of her arm. In fact, the more she spoke the more passion rose in her voice and the tighter her grip became. "Didn't you tell me you were investigating because you wanted justice? If you quit now it will prove you only wanted revenge."

"I don't follow," Eden admitted.

"Justice goes two ways—proving the guilty *and* the innocent. You weren't willing to let Lucas get away with kidnapping and you can't let him get blamed for it if he didn't do it."

Eden jerked away, red finger marks lining her arm.

"I'm sorry!" Ashley tried to rub away the fingers marks on Eden's arm. She wanted to be mad at Ashley, but on one level she knew Ashley was right.

She continued. "Lucas is just a pawn. The mayor is using him to shield his activities. And if Lucas gets caught up in this he could lose his chance at a baseball scholarship."

"He isn't just a pawn. He made a choice to take money from the mayor."

"Yes, but you don't know what kind of pressure the mayor put on him to accept the deal. Maybe he didn't want to do it. Maybe he doesn't realize the long-term ramifications of his decision."

Ashley had a big heart, but Eden was stubborn. "I tell you what. You believe in God, don't you?"

"Of course! You know I do."

"If God gives me a sign, I'll stay on the case." Surely Ashley couldn't argue with such a plan.

Ashley didn't buy into it. "God doesn't need to give signs when He's already made it clear what the right thing to do is."

Okay, Ashley was a bit stubborn too. Eden knew she needed to get out of there before Ashley wore her down. It was time to start her summer vacation. Time to relax.

"Ashley, I'll think about it, I promise." Even though she had no intention of thinking about it other than to confirm her decision to do nothing. "I need to get going."

She had already turned to make for the closest door—the front one—when she stopped short and her heart skipped. Lucas walked past the front window.

She quickly turned to make for the back door, but staring directly at her with a large grin on her face was Ashley.

Now Eden knew what she had to do, but she had no more desire to do it. She spun around, slipped out the front door, and hustled down the sidewalk.

Eden caught up with Lucas at the convenience store. He dropped his head and pretended he didn't see her. She wouldn't let that dissuade her.

She leaned against his car door until he acknowledged her.

He spoke softly. "I thought you agreed you'd leave me alone today."

"Yeah, yeah." Eden waved his words away. "We need to talk. You're in trouble."

He looked around suspiciously, then firmly grabbed her arm. "Let's go for a walk." He seemed scared and wasn't hurting her, so she followed. He led her across the street before releasing her arm. He walked along the sidewalk down Main Street.

Eden wanted to talk, not walk. "Where are you going?"

"There's a walking path along the river. I don't want anyone to hear us." She followed, her curiosity beating out her better judgment.

He was not the guy who'd called her an idiot at The Pizza Parlor or had gone out of his way to call her a wallflower. This Lucas was timid, nervous, maybe even frightened.

They crossed the railroad tracks. The levee was a block ahead. Eden had seen it many times but had never been on it. As they walked up the steps, she heard the flowing river. When they reached the top, she stopped.

The scenery was breathtaking. Upstream, the forked river came together. A hundred feet wide at this point, the river flowed underneath a suspended wooden bridge, down a six-foot waterfall, and underneath an overpass before it curved south and out of sight. Lush green grass filled the short field between the river and the levee. Across the river was a small park dominated by a stage with bleachers.

"What is it?" Lucas asked when he noticed she had stopped.

"It's gorgeous," Eden said in awe.

"Oh, yeah, I guess it is."

When Eden continued to stare at the sight, Lucas offered, "They shot a movie here once, back in the fifties. It was called *Picnic*, I think."

Eden resumed walking.

On the other side of the levee sat an empty baseball field and a swimming pool full of screaming kids, but she didn't take her eyes off of the river's beauty until they'd passed the fork and the line of trees blocked her view.

"Why are you still bothering me?"

"I know you were at the hospital Saturday night. I think you delivered something to the mayor and the doctor for the project they're working on. I know Mayor Washburn wants you to take the blame for Dr. Emmet's disappearance, but I don't know why."

"So you've decided I wasn't responsible for his disappearance now?"

Eden bit her lip. It was hard to admit she had been wrong. "Yes. Although, I know I saw something in your trunk that night. I just don't think it was Dr. Emmet anymore."

"I thought you were ready to lock me up and throw away the key," Lucas joked.

"I'd still like to," Eden admitted. "But I don't think I can."

"Look. I appreciate you admitting you were wrong about me—"

Eden grabbed his arm and tugged so they both stopped to face each other. "I was wrong that you kidnapped Dr. Emmet. After you yelled at me in The Pizza Parlor and I saw whatever I saw in your trunk, I was determined to crucify you. I still want to, but the facts are telling me differently. Let's be clear: I don't like you." She pressed her finger into his chest to accentuate the point. His solid chest.

"I have a confession," Lucas said. "My friend David said he tripped you. That's why you fell and spilled the food and ruined my shoes."

He took off walking again.

She gasped and jogged to catch up. "So *that's* why you eased up on me this morning. You could have just said you were sorry."

He pounded his fist into an open hand. "I didn't say I was sorry," Lucas shot back. He stopped so Eden did too and they faced each other again. "You've been after me ever since that moment. Yes, I shouldn't have said all those things about you, but the way you've judged me made me glad I did."

"Well, I can't say I'm sorry about anything I've said or done. I think you deserve it all."

"Fine!"

"Fine!"

They resumed walking after several moments of awkward silence. They reached the end of the walk, and Lucas turned around and headed back the way they'd come. Eden quietly followed at a distance for a couple of minutes before rejoining him.

"Let's get back to the case. You can't admit to doing something you didn't do."

"The fact is I was there that night and I am going to be accused of kidnapping Dr. Emmet. I'll confess. That's what needs to happen."

"I know Mayor Washburn is paying you a lot of money to be the fall guy."

"It's enough to pay off my car. And he promised to pay for my first year of college."

Wow!

Eden understood. Her mom worked two jobs to make ends meet. She would sure love to have a car and a year of college tuition handed to her.

"You can't trust Jessica and Mayor Washburn. You could end up in jail for a long time."

Lucas waited until a lady pushing a stroller passed by. "They said it will all blow over in a few days."

"What if Dr. Emmet doesn't come back? What if he *can't* come back?"

Lucas stopped. "What are you saying?"

"Jessica and the mayor are up to something big, and I get the creepy feeling they will do anything to succeed. What if the police find *evidence*," Eden emphasized her point with air quotation marks, "against you that puts you away longer than a few days?"

"That seems a little far-fetched."

Eden heard a tiny doubt in his voice. "Maybe. Even if it does blow over in a few days, what if it lasts long enough for you to miss your baseball competition? Or what if a college doesn't want to offer a baseball scholarship to someone mixed up in possible kidnapping or murder charges?"

"But…I…"

Eden didn't know if his hesitation to speak was from doubt or the pair of joggers nearing them. They walked in silence until the joggers passed.

"Those are the best case scenarios," Eden continued. "You may beat kidnapping or murder charges legally, but this will scar your reputation unless you prove yourself to be innocent. And if you confess, well, it's going to end badly for you."

She used her hand to stop Lucas and turn him so she could look into his eyes. "Look, I know what it's like to take the blame for something I didn't do.

"My friends and I went skiing in Colorado over spring break. One of them was driving home in heavy rain when she swerved to miss a deer, causing another car to roll into a ditch.

"She panicked and drove a few miles before we calmed her down enough to stop.

"I didn't know, but she had purchased jelly beans laced with marijuana and had eaten some.

"Another one of my friends called 9-1-1 while I drove the car back to the scene of the accident. There was already a state trooper on the scene. We hadn't realized he was behind us and saw the accident and us leave. The policeman saw me drive up so I told him I had been driving when the accident occurred. I didn't want my friend to get into trouble for driving while high. I mean, it was an accident—no big deal, right?

"He ticketed me for leaving the scene of the crime as well as reckless driving, then they searched the vehicle and found the drugs. We all got nailed for possession.

"I had saved for three years so I could go to Disneyworld for a graduation trip, but instead I spent all that money on fines and a lawyer, trying to minimize the damage. I could have gotten jail time but my mom pleaded with the judge to go easy since it was my first offense.

"I ended up with probation on the stipulation that I spend the summer living with my grandma and not having any contact with my three best friends.

"So go ahead and take the blame for something you didn't do, but don't think some cop or judge won't screw up your future plans."

They resumed walking and Lucas stared straight ahead, ignoring Eden.

They had reached the fork again so she focused on the river.

"Llama."

"What?" Eden asked, confused.

"I had a llama in my trunk."

"What were you doing with a llama? Aren't they large?"

"It wasn't a full-grown llama, and I got it for Mayor Washburn; for Dr. Emmet's experiments."

"Where did you get a llama?"

Lucas sighed and pointed. "There's an animal farm northwest of here, about thirty miles. I stole it."

"You stole a llama and stuffed it in your trunk?" Eden was horrified.

"That's mostly what I've done for them—steal animals."

"So you *are* a kidnapper!"

Lucas shrugged. "I guess."

"You guess! You can't just take other people's animals."

Lucas got defensive. "I didn't say I was proud of it. Besides, they pay well. How do you think I could afford the payments for my car?"

They sat on a concrete bench with the waterfall for a view. "What are they doing with the animals?"

"I don't know," Lucas admitted. "Most of the time they give them back."

"What?"

"When they're done I take them back where I took them from."

Eden laughed. She couldn't help it. The sight of Lucas returning a stolen animal was pure comedy. "How long do they keep the animals?"

"Sometimes a few days. Sometimes a week or two."

Eden laughed even harder now. "Can you imagine the face of someone when their llama is returned after it's been missing for two weeks?"

Lucas joined her laughter. "One time I took a dog from a backyard. It was a very friendly boxer. Two days later I saw signs up all over town. The boxer belonged to an eight-year-old girl. I felt so bad that when I returned the dog I attached a note and a hundred-dollar bill to her collar."

"Oh my gosh, that's so sweet!"

"I'm not all bad," Lucas said.

Eden gave him a sidelong glance. "Maybe not."

Lucas looked down, his head resting on his hands. After a few moments he mumbled something to himself, stood, and made his way back toward the convenience store and his car. He kept punching his fist into his hand and mumbling.

Eden followed at a distance until they neared his car, then determined to push him for an answer before he got away. "I know it's a hard decision, but you are short on time."

"The mayor will want his money back," Lucas lamented.

"Yes he will."

"*If* I decide not to take the fall, how do you suggest I proceed?" Lucas looked at her almost pleadingly.

Eden contemplated. "We need to search the doctor's lab but I've had a hard time getting past Jessica."

"I know how to get in. There's a white door in back that's rusted. Even though it's locked, if you pull just right it will open."

"Perfect. I think you should leave town for a few hours. Don't let the police find you. Then meet me at the hospital later tonight, say around ten-thirty."

"Even if I hide, I'm going to get blamed for what happened to Dr. Emmet," Lucas said.

"I know, but it will buy us some time to figure out what really happened."

"What do you hope to find at the hospital?" he asked.

"I don't know," Eden admitted. "But there's something strange going on in there and we need to figure out what."

Chapter 14

Mayor Washburn had been so worried about media at the City Council meeting that Eden decided to attend. She arrived a few minutes early, surprised to see only two other people.

A lady from the local newspaper, *The Harvey County Independent,* introduced herself to Eden as the editor of the newspaper. She asked Eden if she was new to town—maybe she'd put it in the paper so Eden wouldn't have to answer that question again—and how she liked working at The Pizza Parlor.

Mayor Washburn would be relieved at the lack of media coverage, something he'd seemed very concerned about earlier.

The crowd reached six by the time the meeting started. Besides herself and two reporters, the other attendees were an elderly lady and two middle-aged men, all sitting separately. A young lady sat behind a video camera set up to record the meeting for a local public television station.

Mayor Washburn was perched behind a long podium with two council-members seated on either side of him. Farther to his left were two seats with name plates for the attorney and the treasurer. The mayor appeared anxious when Eden arrived, as anxious as he had sounded when she'd overheard him talking to Jessica. When he called the meeting to order, she thought he looked more like the relaxed, laid-back man she'd met at Mrs. Emmet's house.

As the meeting started, Officer Dirks stepped inside and stood next to the door. The mayor went through several formal procedures, including approval of last week's minutes and the payment of the current bills. The two men in attendance each gave department reports to the council and then exited. That left Eden, the elderly lady, and the reporter as the lone observers.

Eden had expected the meeting to be exciting, or at least interesting. She wanted desperately to leave but didn't want everyone to watch her, so she sat and endured as the mayor and the city council droned on and on about boring city business. At one point she pulled out her phone and tried to play a game, but one of the council members scowled at her so she put it away. She soon found herself tuning out and reciting pizza ingredient lists. Boy, was she bored!

She snapped back into the moment when she heard Mayor Washburn ask, "Is there any new business from the public?"

The lady in the front row raised her hand.

Mayor Washburn smiled. "Yes, Mrs. Prescott. You may approach the podium and address the council."

Mrs. Prescott, who looked old enough to be Maimeo's mother, laboriously stood with significant help from her cane. One of the council-members helped her walk to the podium and adjusted the microphone so she could reach it.

"I—I heard that that nice Dr. Emmet is missing." She paused and stuttered and had a general look of frustration about her, as if her mind knew what it wanted to say but her mouth could not cooperate.

The council waited for more, but Mrs. Prescott looked at them expectantly. Finally Mayor Washburn said, "I don't know where Dr. Emmet is at this moment."

She leaned again toward the microphone. "Did someone take him?"

Mayor Washburn looked a bit off kilter. "Um, the police are looking into the matter."

"Can the police stop by and check on my Elmer?"

"Wh-what's that, Mrs. Prescott?" the mayor asked.

"If someone is out there stealing men, I want to know my son's okay."

Eden stifled a laugh. "I saw Elmer outside his barbershop this afternoon," Mayor Washburn said patiently. "I assure you he was doing just fine."

"O-okay. Th-thank you."

One of the council-members helped Mrs. Prescott to the door and Officer Dirks escorted her out.

The council talked about plans for Old Settlers Days, which happened sometime in August, though Eden didn't catch the exact date.

It seemed like they were about to wrap up when the door burst open. Everyone jumped.

It was Sam Nelson.

"Is that goddamned mayor here?"

He reeked of alcohol and held a beer bottle in his right hand, which he pointed at the mayor. "I know you know I know where." He stopped and rolled his eyes upward like he was thinking exceptionally hard. Then he spoke one word at a time. "I know you know where Dr. Emmet is."

Mayor Washburn looked befuddled. The council had all stood when Sam entered but seemed uncertain as to what to do, and hesitant to approach with him swinging the bottle wildly around.

Sam noticed the television camera and decided to address his grievance to the world. He gradually moved toward the camera as he spoke. "Twenty years ago today, Dr. Emmet killed my son. Mayor Washburn was there; he knows the truth. And now the doctor is hiding." He tried to make quotation marks with his fingers but found it awfully difficult and finally abandoned the gesture. He bent over and stared at the video camera, now mere inches from his face. "Dr. Emmet and the mayor are hiding the doctor and I can't find him. They're both cowards!" He turned and pointed the bottle at Mayor Washburn and screamed, "Tell me where he is or else!"

With Sam's attention on the mayor, one of the council members, a big, burly guy, snuck around behind Sam and grabbed him from behind in a bear hug. The drunk struggled but the big man was stronger and in much better condition. He held tight and patiently waited for Sam to calm down. Sam's body relaxed as he began to weep. The council member took the bottle from Sam and handed it to another of the council-members.

"There, there. It's all going to be okay. You just need a good night's rest."

Chapter 15

After the city council meeting, Eden walked the block and a half to the hospital. The black SUV—Eden assumed that meant Jessica was there—was parked outside the front entrance. She found a spot across the street, underneath a tree, to watch and wait. Shortly after her, Mayor Washburn passed the black SUV on foot and entered the hospital. She could see light from within when the mayor opened the door.

She wondered if Lucas had left town or if he had changed his mind. He knew how to get in the back, so she rooted for the former.

She watched a squirrel scamper down a nearby tree and stop near her. It stood on its hind legs and stared straight at her. The street lights quickly dimmed then went out. She lost her visual on the squirrel, but heard it flee up the tree. The outside flood lights on the hospital had also gone out. Down the block in both directions houses were dark. She checked her phone—nine-thirty.

What was this all about? There wasn't a cloud in the sky, and the wind was light. A few seconds later they came back on.

The next hour was uneventful. How could detectives survive the boredom of stakeouts? To start with they probably don't sit through two hours of a boring small town business meeting, though she had to admit the few minutes of Sam barging in and threatening Mayor Washburn had made the torture worth it.

She checked her phone. Almost ten-thirty. As she walked around to the south side of the hospital where Lucas had suggested they meet, she noticed a blue-ish light on the fourth floor and wondered if that was the lab. Hopefully the mayor wasn't up there! She paced up and down the alley, the same alley she had watched Mayor Washburn give Lucas money, as ten-thirty turned into ten-forty.

Eden gave up on Lucas, found the rusted, white metal door, and yanked. "Lucas told me you would open, even though you're locked." She yanked again. "But you're not cooperating." She placed her foot flat on the wall and pulled, involuntarily letting out a grunt. Then she tried the other foot. Same result.

She bent over to catch her breath. Checked her phone again. Ten-forty-five. She couldn't try the front door again. She shook her arms and placed her foot once again flat on the wall. "Okay, you're about to see how stubborn I can be." She gritted her teeth and grunted.

"I think I've already seen that."

Eden screamed and turned, slamming her back against the door.

Lucas rushed toward her and threw his hand over her mouth to stifle the scream, while he carefully cradled a dark cat with his other arm. Both he and the cat had fear in their eyes.

She slapped his arm. "You frightened me to death."

"I thought you knew I was here."

"If I knew you were here I would have said hello. You're late," she scolded.

"Hey, I'm a fugitive. I couldn't just park my car at the hospital. I had to hide it."

"What have you been doing the last few hours?" Eden asked.

"Nothing."

"So you couldn't have parked fifteen minutes early to get here on time?"

"You said ten-thirty, so that's when I parked my... Ohhh! I see what you mean."

Eden rolled her eyes.

The cat meowed and buried its head into Lucas's neck. He rubbed his face against the animal and was rewarded with a lick.

Eden gagged. "How can you let that cat lick you? It's disgusting."

"She's purrrty." He smiled, "Get it? Purrr—."

"I get it," she huffed.

"And she's a kitten, not a cat." He scratched her belly and she purred in delight.

The whiskers, dark brown eyes, and pointy ears with hair growing inside like an old man's, what was cute about the beast? If it weighed a hundred pounds instead of three it would be trying to eat Lucas, not just lick him.

No, there was nothing attractive about the stray.

She tried to ignore the love fest. "Jessica's car is out front, so I assume she's inside. I saw Mayor Washburn enter the hospital at eight fifty-three. No one has come or gone since then. At nine-thirty exactly all the lights went out for a few moments, then came back on. At ten twenty-six, while I walked around the building so I could be here *on time*," she paused, hoping Lucas would catch the jab, "I noticed a light on the fourth floor."

"When the lights went out, did they go out kind of slow then come back on all of a sudden?" Lucas asked.

"Yeah, why?"

"That happens a lot around here," Lucas explained. "Some people have complained to the city council and they asked the electric company, who said it was just too much electricity being used at one time. It only happens for a few seconds and the lights always come back on, so the electric company and the city council can't do much about it. Some people think it has to do with Dr. Emmet and the hospital."

"But he's not here. Unless the mayor's in the lab." She patted the door. "Isn't this the door you can get into?"

"You're not still thinking about going in there, are you?" Lucas said, full of concern.

"Of course we are," Eden said. "How else are we going to figure out what's going on?"

"We? I told you I don't like it in there. There's... there's ghosts and things."

"If you're so afraid of ghosts, why are you carrying around a black cat?"

"She's not black. She's gray." He shined his phone's flashlight close to her fur, proving his point.

"Anyhow, I told you there's no such thing as ghosts," Eden retorted. "Let's go inside and I'll prove it to you."

Lucas gave her a look of disbelief but didn't argue further. "This door is locked but if you..."

Lucas handed the cat to Eden, who was so caught off guard she accepted it.

"...if you pull up hard," which he demonstrated as he spoke, "then it pops right open."

Eden set the cat down before Lucas finished with the door.

"What are you doing?" Lucas squatted down on one knee and retrieved the kitten.

"That thing can't go inside."

"She's one of my favorite strays. Always friendly and cuddly. And she's lonely."

Lucas looked hurt, but Eden stood her ground.

They switched their phones onto flashlight mode and Lucas made sure the door latched shut behind them.

Eden shined her light on a big island in the middle of the room with pots and pans hanging above. There were containers on the counter, a commercial-size refrigerator, and aprons hanging from a nail. She ran her finger across the top of the island. Except for the thick dust, the kitchen looked ready to use.

Lucas pointed. "The stairs are that way."

"You should lead the way," Eden suggested.

"I'm not going first!"

She chuckled. "You finally said something I believe."

With Lucas behind her, Eden wove through the kitchen and pushed the two-way door, which opened into another large room of darkness. She circled around the dining room serving line, then carefully weaved through the round tables, complete with chairs. Lucas stayed so close behind Eden that she could smell the spearmint gum he chomped on.

Eden felt Lucas's hand on her shoulder. She shrugged it off, but he grabbed her again, this time with more force. What a chicken.

"Wait!" He whispered desperately. "Did you hear that?"

She stopped and listened. Nothing.

Lucas pointed his phone to their left, two tables away. Eden's gaze followed the light. She had heard nothing, now she saw nothing.

"Come on, you big baby."

"I-I know I heard something."

"Your mind is playing tricks on you."

Eden continued on. She felt a tug on the bottom of her shirt. It took her a second to realize it was Lucas.

"Are you holding onto my shirt?"

"Um, I don't want you to get lost."

She only managed another step before Lucas yanked hard, choking her with the neckline. She slapped his hand away. Lucas pointed his light underneath another table. "I heard it again."

"There's nothing over there."

"I know what I heard," he insisted.

Frustrated, Eden marched to the table and squatted, shining her phone's light underneath.

"What are you doing?" He took a step toward her, then retreated, having an obvious dilemma between the comfort of her presence and the fear of the sound.

Eden stood. "There's nothing here."

"Of course not. Y-You can't see ghosts."

"Then why did you shine your light this direction?"

"I was hoping it *wasn't* a ghost."

"I've told you, there are no such things as ghosts. Now, can we continue on?"

Suddenly the chair beside Lucas moved. He leapt onto the table, rolled across, and tumbled off the other side, his flailing arm slapping Eden's phone from her hand and onto the floor.

"Are you okay?" Eden asked out of obligation. Keeping her eyes on the chair that moved, she picked up her phone and cautiously crept toward it.

Lucas untangled himself from the chairs he had landed on, and then scrambled to his feet.

Eden ignored him. She scooped up Lucas's "ghost" and shouted for him to halt as he raced toward the kitchen door.

"Lucas Walls!"

He stopped dead in his tracks. He slowly turned toward Eden.

"Did you let her in here?" Eden held the gray cat in one arm and shined the phone light onto it with her free hand.

"Um, yeah, she wanted to come in," he said quietly.

"Well here's your ghost."

Lucas took the stray from her and petted her with affection. "I can take her back outside."

Eden snatched the cat and set her down. "There's no way I'm letting *you* take her outside. You'll never come back."

When Lucas reached for the cat, Eden grabbed his arm. "Forget the cat. We came here to find out what Dr. Emmet is experimenting on in his lab. Let's try to stay focused."

The cafeteria exited into a long, dark hallway. Eden shined her light down one side, then the other, of the creepy, empty space. At Lucas's direction, she led them to the right, where the hallway ended into a large lobby area containing the first windows Eden had seen since they entered the hospital. The windows lined the far side of the room. The tall, dark blinds were drawn, but still allowed the streetlights outside to illuminate the room enough to see without the use of their phones.

The front of the room held a reception desk with monitors rising above the counter top and two doors on either side of the desk. The waiting area consisted of several rows of chairs and in the back corner a children's area furnished with a train table, a wicker basket full of toys, and a low reading table with Dr. Seuss books spread on top. An open doorway in the back of the room led to the same hallway that contained Jessica's office. Her light was on.

"Let's get out of here quick before Jessica sees us."

Lucas breathed a sigh of relief. "Finally."

She playfully slapped his arm. "I don't mean out of the hospital. Let's get out of this room. Where are the stairs?"

"Oh." Eden thought he had been joking, but apparently not.

"The stairs are that way." Lucas nudged Eden toward the door on the other side of the room.

As soon as Eden opened the door, the streetlights outside dimmed then went dark. Lucas grabbed her arm and pain shot through her. She slammed his hand with her phone and he let go. "Ouch!"

Eden slapped her hand over his mouth. "Shh!" She looked back and saw that Jessica's office light was off. Without much of a moon to shine in from the outside, the lobby was completely dark. She quickly stepped through the doorway and quietly shut the door.

"What was that for?"

"You were hurting my arm," Eden said through clenched teeth. "I didn't want to yell at you because Jessica would have heard. I hit you instead of yelling because I'm trying to keep us from being arrested for breaking and entering."

Lucas wouldn't let it go. "If I can't pitch next weekend then the scouts won't see me and I could lose an opportunity for a scholarship."

Eden glared at him, anger coursing through her veins. "If you're in jail for kidnapping or murder, scouts can't watch you pitch either."

He glared at her but wisely kept his mouth shut.

Lucas pointed his light on an overhead sign marking the stairway.

Eden quickly slapped the phone from Lucas's hand and it slammed onto the hard, tiled floor and went dark.

"Hey, what was that for?"

"You've got to leave the light off or Jessica will see us," Eden scolded. "There's a window in the door."

Eden peeked out through the window into the darkness while Lucas crawled on the ground, groping for his phone.

Suddenly Jessica's light came back on and Eden instinctively ducked.

"I can't get my phone to turn on. I think you broke it."

"Worry about that later. As long as we have one light we'll be fine."

Eden felt her way along the wall until she reached the far door. She pushed through the door and when Lucas was through, she let it shut. The clank from the door echoed around and above. Eden turned the light back on her phone, revealing concrete stairs that zigzagged upward.

"This isn't my phone."

"What?" Eden shined the light onto the phone Lucas held in his hand—her phone.

He chuckled. "You broke your own phone."

How? They must have gotten switched in the cafeteria when he sprawled across the table. She handed Lucas his phone and shoved hers into her pocket. "Now you have the light; lead the way."

He quickly handed his phone back to her. "You can use mine for now."

She pointed the light downward and carefully navigated each step, holding tightly to the metal railing. They walked up the four flights of stairs in silence.

The carpet lining the long, wide hallway on the fourth floor didn't look anything like the other carpets Eden had seen in the hospital. Everywhere else the carpets were clean, but this carpet had holes, strings frayed in spots, stains, and spots of dirt and dried mud. The doors along the hallway were all closed.

One room about halfway down had a blue glowing light seeping underneath the door. Lucas pointed toward it and backed up until he was against the wall. "Th-Th-That's the room where the ghost lives"

"What do you mean?"

"The room with the goat. That's the room where the goat appeared."

Exasperated, she said, "You do realize you were the one who brought the goat to the hospital, don't you?"

"I know, but, but it hadn't been in the room when I checked the first time. And then it just was."

Eden looked at him like he was an idiot, which she was becoming more and more convinced of.

"Goats don't just appear. Now come on!" She grabbed his arm and pulled. He reluctantly followed.

Eden quietly opened the door and peered into the room. She flipped the light switch and the overhead light came on. The room reminded her of the one in which her cousin got his X-ray taken when he broke his arm two years ago. The left side of the room, where the door entered, was empty. The back wall on that side of the room had double windows to the outside with blinds pulled down.

A large machine, emitting a constant hum similar to a refrigerator, filled the right side of the room. The center of the machine contained a round tunnel six feet long and four wide, and glass or plastic ends to enclose it. The top reached the eight-foot ceiling.

The glowing blue light they had seen came from the monitor attached to the machine. The current date and time were in the top left corner: May 15, 2021, 10:59 pm. The rest of the screen contained indiscernible numbers scrolling across.

She snapped a photo using Lucas's phone.

"Does any of this make sense to you?" she asked Lucas.

"It's a data log. Tells the activity of the machine and that it's in good, functional order."

"But it doesn't say what it does?"

"No," Lucas admitted. He opened another door on the side of the room. "There's another room connected to this one."

The small office contained an old wood desk in the middle with a relatively newer padded chair behind it. The only thing on the desk was a half-full cup of coffee.

Eden felt it. "It's still warm." The white mug contained an image of the hospital and said 1902-2002 underneath the picture. Eden snapped a picture with her cell phone.

"We'd better get out of here!" Lucas urged.

Eden waved him off. "Hang on a minute."

Behind the desk was a single bookshelf. The top shelf was empty, but a set of medicine books lined the second shelf. The third shelf held a microwave oven and a cup of stir sticks. The bottom shelf had two stacks of medical journals.

Eden handed one stack of the journals to Lucas. "Flip through these and see if anything looks unusual."

He took the first journal and fanned through the pages. Eden did likewise with the other stack.

"What am I looking for?" Lucas asked.

"I don't know. Anything that looks like it's out of place."

They finished about the same time but neither of them found anything helpful. Eden carefully put them back in place.

"Let's leave. We're running out of time."

Eden ignored him. "One more place we need to look." She opened each of the drawers of the desk but only found items she would expect to find: a stapler, ruler, paperclips and pens.

She hated to leave; she had expected to find a breakthrough clue tonight.

Lucas pleaded again. "It's time to go."

"Wait!" Eden exclaimed. "What did you say?"

"I said we have to go. Whoever is drinking that coffee will be back any moment."

"No, no. What did you say before that?"

Lucas really had to think. "We're running out of time?"

She snapped her fingers. "That was it!" She pulled the twenty-dollar bill that Dr. Emmet had given her two nights before from her pocket. "That's it!" She jumped up and down. "Lucas, I know what happened!"

"Good, can we get out of here?"

"Yes. I can't wait to tell Officer Dirks what really happened to Dr. Emmet!" Eden said gleefully.

Chapter 16

The next morning Eden ran the whole way to the hospital. Well, walked really quickly. She knew it was a risky move—to sneak back into the hospital—when there was no certainty that her theory was right. But she had to take another look at the machine before she told Officer Dirks. If she was right, this would be her last opportunity to see it.

Fortunately, she didn't see Jessica's Black SUV in the parking lot, so Eden popped open the back door and retraced her and Lucas's journey through the hospital from the night before. She gazed longingly at the roughly four hundred cubic feet of amazing technology. Eden ran her hand along the side as affectionately as Lucas had petted the kitten the night before. Goosebumps rose on her arms and up her neck as she thought about standing in this little, unknown town in the middle of the country, touching a machine that would change the course of human history.

Ironically, she lost track of time.

She had to share what she knew with the police. She would never see the machine again once they knew what it did.

As she started to leave, the door to the attached office, which had been ajar, creaked open a few more inches. She wasn't alone.

Her heart pounded as she debated her options. Whoever was in the room wanted privacy. But why push the door open to see? Why not wait quietly until she left? When she asked herself if it could be Dr. Emmet, she stepped forward and cautiously pushed the door open.

The only noticeable difference being the missing coffee cup, she crept toward the desk. A cat leapt from behind the desk and Eden jumped. That stupid cat that Lucas had let into the hospital the night before. She nudged her head against Eden's thigh. She glared down at the cat, resisting an urge deep within her to pet the cat so maybe it would stop staring at her. She ignored the kitten.

Eden's eyes told her everything was the same, but her emotions screamed something was wrong; even more wrong than the presence of the cat. The shades were closed but the overhead light from the lab was enough to see by. Still, Eden felt uncomfortable in the dimness, so she made for the window to invite the sunshine in.

Her foot caught and she tumbled to the ground clumsily, just like she had in The Pizza Parlor when she'd spilled spaghetti all over Lucas.

Then another similarity between the two accidents caused her to shriek. She had been tripped by a foot.

Beside her lay the dead body of Mayor Washburn.

Chapter 17

*L*ess than five minutes after Eden found Mayor Washburn's body, Officer Johnson arrived, Jessica right on his heels. Two minutes later Lucas showed up, followed by Officer Dirks, out of uniform wearing jeans and a Halstead Dragons t-shirt. Officer Dirks gave instructions to a young woman sporting an expensive looking camera. She began taking photos of everything. They found Eden sitting on the floor with her head leaning against the machine.

She desperately wanted to cry. She had never seen a dead body. She had only been to one funeral—her great-uncle Harvey when she was ten—but it had been a closed casket. She couldn't get the image of the mayor's lifeless body out of her mind.

As they each arrived, Eden simply pointed toward the next room. Lucas asked her how she was doing. She stared forward, ignoring the question. How could she possibly articulate how she felt? To his credit, Lucas sat next to her and kept his mouth shut. And thankfully he held the kitten who hadn't left her side since discovering the body.

Jessica wept loudly in the next room before rushing through the lab and into the hallway, her sobs quickly fading from earshot.

After a while Lucas patted Eden's knee. "I'm going to go talk to Mickey. I'm here if you need me."

Lucas stood in the doorway and spoke with Mickey. Eden tuned them out. She didn't want to hear any more about the corpse.

Except, she heard talk of Dr. Emmet and her ears perked up.

It was Officer Johnson speaking to Officer Dirks, with Lucas hovering nearby. "Maybe that's why Dr. Emmet went missing."

"Could Dr. Emmet be hiding in order to set up the murder?" Officer Dirks shook his head. "It's possible."

"Dr. Emmet couldn't have done it." Eden stood, her legs still shaking more than she would like.

"Eden figured out what happened to Dr. Emmet," Lucas informed the two officers with complete confidence, even though she hadn't yet told him her theory.

"Miss Price, I'd love to hear what you know."

It was tough, given the circumstances, but Eden looked at the machine and slowly felt a twinge of her previous excitement return. She proclaimed triumphantly, "Dr. Emmet couldn't have murdered Mayor Washburn because he's traveling through time."

Chapter 18

Lucas and Mickey burst into laughter. Officer Dirks couldn't help himself and chortled.

Eden stood beside the machine's monitor and answered defensively. "It makes perfect sense! That's why the animals disappeared without a trace. That's why Lucas saw a goat suddenly appear: because it arrived from the past. That's why Mrs. Emmet thought she slept for nine days. She had only slept one night but was transported ahead in time nine days. That's why the lights go on and off—from a power surge when the time machine is used."

"What are you talking about?" Officer Dirks asked as the other two continued to roar with laughter.

"Mrs. Emmet told me how the medicine she takes makes her sleep. In fact, she said that one time she had slept for nine days. At first I thought she was exaggerating, but then I read in Sam Nelson's journal that he saw Dr. Emmet and Mayor Washburn take her to the hospital and the doctor and Mrs. Emmet didn't come out for nine days. What could they have been doing? Sam wrote in his journal that the day they returned home he knocked on their door and Mrs. Emmet answered, but she had no signs of bandages and seemed in a normal state of mind. I admit I was as confused about it as Sam."

A flash caused her to pause and glare at the lady with the camera that had interrupted her explanation. She quickly regrouped.

"He also wrote in his journal that Mayor Washburn and Dr. Emmet often took animals into the hospital. Several times Sam snuck into the hospital after they left but never found the animals. Lucas told me he saw a goat in the lab, but he had just been in the lab and it had been empty.

"I knew there had to be something strange going on in this room, I just couldn't figure out what—until last night." Eden pulled out the twenty-dollar bill from her pocket. "The last clue that helped me figure out what happened was the first clue I had. Dr. Emmet gave me this the night he disappeared. He had circled some of the letters."

"Right," Officer Dirks cut in. "They said 'item machine,' if I remember correctly."

"That's almost right," Eden agreed. "But if you rearrange the letters in the first word you get 'time machine.' I don't think anyone took Dr. Emmet. I think he invented a time machine and is testing it himself."

Mickey and Lucas had stopped laughing to listen to Eden's explanation. They were trying not to laugh further, but having a hard time of it.

"If that were true," Officer Dirks surmised, "couldn't Dr. Emmet be anywhere in time? And couldn't he have come back to the same moment he left so no one would ever know he was gone?"

Eden shook her head emphatically. "You're thinking science fiction. Time travel to the past isn't possible, but time travel into the future is."

"Do you have any solid evidence to support your claim?" Officer Johnson asked.

"On the bill that Dr. Emmet gave me he wrote 'she knows.' I think the 'she' is Jessica Barns, and I bet she can tell you this is a time machine."

"We'll be sure to ask her about it," Officer Johnson said, the sarcasm not subtle.

Officer Dirks gave a big sigh. "I think your theory, while creative, is fantastical and wishful thinking."

Eden dug in her heels. "But it's the only thing that makes sense."

"You know things are crazy when the most logical explanation is a time machine," Mickey cracked.

"It would explain the goat," Lucas said thoughtfully.

Officer Dirks didn't budge. "I'll grant you that a lot of things the last few days don't make sense, but neither does a time machine. What I do think makes sense is that you've concocted a crazy theory trying to get Lucas out of trouble." Eden started to protest but he put up his hand to stop her. "We'll investigate thoroughly. We'll ask the questions we need to determine the truth. At this point we need to treat the doctor's disappearance and the mayor's death as two separate occurrences until we find something concrete that links them together. We still don't have any evidence of foul play with Dr. Emmet."

She wanted to argue, but what more could she say? She didn't have any proof.

Officer Dirks turned to Lucas. "I've been looking for you, young man. I need you to answer some questions about the night Dr. Emmet disappeared."

Lucas stuttered, then went quiet. His face was flushed with fear and his body tense. He focused on the kitten and didn't make eye contact with either policeman.

"Why don't you two wait downstairs while we investigate this crime scene. I'll need to interview you both. And if you see Jessica, tell her to stay put because we'll have some questions for her too."

"Yes sir," Eden and Lucas echoed.

As soon as they entered the downstairs lobby, they heard Jessica crying in her office. Lucas sat on the floor, his back against the wall, and played with the kitten. Eden would have to deliver the message to Jessica. She hated to disturb her.

She stood in Jessica's doorway, still undecided, when Jessica snapped, "What do you want?"

Eden contemplated leaving, but she felt sorry for Jessica in spite of the way she had been treated. "I'm sorry about Mayor Washburn. I know you were... close."

Jessica sat behind her desk, behind a pile of boxes. Eden couldn't see her, but heard her blow her nose.

"Officer Dirks asked that you remain here until he asks you some questions."

The crying seemed to dry up a bit. "Okay."

That was all she was going to get out of Jessica. Eden thought it seemed odd. She caught movement in the picture hanging on the wall. Through the reflection she saw Jessica hurriedly open her desk drawer, remove a book and shove it into a handbag. The book had a black cover and a design of some sort on the front, but Eden couldn't make it out in the reflection. Wait, was that a picture of the time machine? On the front of her book?

Jessica scurried out of her office, nearly knocking Eden over in passing, without apologizing, and out of the hospital. She hopped into her SUV and was gone.

Chapter 19

*A*fter answering questions for Officer Johnson and him suggesting they remain available for further questioning, Eden left the hospital with Lucas. She reached into the pocket of her Capri pants before remembering she didn't have her cell phone. She left it at her grandma's house because she broke it last night when she slapped it out of Lucas's hand. That's why she had to run down to Jessica's office to call the police after finding the mayor's body. "What time is it?" she asked Lucas.

He checked his phone. "It's ten forty."

"I have just enough time before work to stop at Mrs. Emmet's and tell her what happened to her husband."

"You're going to tell Mrs. Emmet that her husband invented a time machine and transported himself into the future?"

"She'll want to know he's safe."

"If he's testing a time machine how do you know he's safe?"

"He's already tested it."

Lucas shook his head and mumbled something.

Eden ignored him. "Are you coming with me?"

"Oh, I wouldn't miss this for the world!"

When Mrs. Emmet answered the door, Eden could immediately tell something was amiss. It wasn't the gray turtleneck sweater—though a sweater in this heat seemed odd—but her demeanor. She seemed distracted, and instead of cordially inviting them inside, Mrs. Emmet stepped onto the front porch and closed the door behind her.

"I only have a minute before I need to be at work, but I wanted to stop and tell you that I believe your husband is okay."

Mrs. Emmet perked up. "What? You know where he is?"

"Yes," Eden said confidently. "The machine in his lab is a time machine, and he's traveled into the future." Eden bit her lower lip. "Only... I don't know how far into the future he traveled."

"Eden, this isn't funny!"

Eden was taken aback. She'd expected excitement from Mrs. Emmet, maybe even a thank you. She wanted to push her point, but couldn't be late for work and Mrs. Emmet's ears were red. Eden had clearly upset her.

She had another idea. "I think you should ask Jessica about it. I saw her hide a book with a picture of the machine on it. She snuck it out of the hospital in her bag. I think she knows all about it."

Eden shifted uncomfortably. Why didn't Mrs. Emmet say anything? Her eyes darted around nervously. Eden felt horrible. She had clearly upset Mrs. Emmet, which had not been her intention.

"I'm sorry. I know it's a lot to process. But I'm sure that's where he is. I can tell you more when you're ready."

"I need to go," Mrs. Emmet said shortly and disappeared into her house.

"You forgot to tell her about Mayor Washburn," Lucas noted.

"I'll let someone she knows better tell her that her and her husband's good friend is dead."

As they started toward The Pizza Parlor, Eden noticed Mrs. Emmet pull out of her garage.

"I wonder where she's going," Lucas said.

How badly had Eden upset her? She placed her hand on Lucas's arm. "Do me a favor, will you?"

"Sure, okay."

"Follow Mrs. Emmet and make sure she gets to wherever she's going, okay. I'm worried about her. Then let me know."

Once again Eden ran to work.

Chapter 20

*E*den was starting to resent the new cash register. It was more sophisticated than this small restaurant needed, and with Ashley still learning how to use it, Eden was stuck washing dishes. Ugh! She didn't always get along too well with technology, but working the front counter was better than any of these other lame jobs.

Her stomach growled. She hadn't had time to eat before work and the smell of the fresh breadsticks in the oven made her mouth water. The dark-haired busboy set a tub of dirty dishes with half-eaten food on the counter. Eden mourned for the pepperoni and mushroom slice with only a single bite missing.

When the lunch crowd thinned, Ashley joined her in the kitchen. "I did some research. Back in 1999, Sam sued Dr. Emmet for the negligence and murder of his son. Sam had to be removed from the court several times and was charged with contempt once. At first they had a hung jury, but the judge sent the jurors back to deliberation until they returned with a not guilty verdict. When the verdict was read, Sam became so vulgar and violent he was arrested and spent several days in jail until he cooled down."

Eden didn't have any trouble believing Sam was capable of seeking his vengeance for what had happened to his son. After what she had read in his journal, she was surprised he hadn't done something much earlier.

The front door rang. Ashley went to the counter to help and Eden followed.

Jessica had rebounded; there was no sign of her crying fit from earlier. She had showered and changed from sweats to gray pants and a white blouse.

"I'm here to pick up my order."

Eden found Jessica's sandwich in a to-go sack and took it to Ashley.

"Ah, Price. I'm sure you've heard by now."

Eden didn't have a clue what Jessica meant. "Heard what?"

"The police arrested Sam Nelson for Gaylord's murder." Her biting tone accentuated her contempt. "He's also the prime suspect in Dr. Emmet's disappearance. They don't have much hope of finding the doctor alive." She showed no sadness when she spoke of Dr. Emmet.

"I hadn't heard."

"I guess the police figured this one out without you."

Jessica grabbed her lunch and disappeared out the front door.

"What do you think?" Ashley asked Eden.

"Well, first of all, Dr. Emmet will show up again. I just don't know when."

Eden explained to Ashley her theory on the time machine. Ashley grew increasingly excited. "That's incredible!"

"It is! But I can't prove it. And it has nothing to do with the mayor's murder."

"Do you think Sam killed the mayor?"

"I don't know. It makes sense. Sam hated Dr. Emmet. And he also hated the mayor," Eden said as she remembered his outburst at the city council meeting.

"You sound like you have a bit of doubt."

"Why now? I mean, I get that it's the twentieth anniversary and all, but what about the previous nineteen anniversaries?"

"Oh, that's what I started to tell you before we got interrupted. After the trial, Sam left Halstead. In fact, he left Kansas. He lived in Texas, I believe, until last year, when he moved back to town."

"Why did Sam come back now?" Eden wondered aloud.

"I don't know. Do you want me to try and find out?"

"No, it doesn't matter."

"Are you going to keep investigating?" Ashley asked, sounding hopeful.

Eden shook her head. "No way. Even if the police don't believe me, *I* know where Dr. Emmet is. I've been looking for an excuse to quit messing with this since I found out Lucas didn't do it. Now that he's in the clear, I'm going to relax and enjoy my afternoon and kick off my summer vacation. Back to Plan A for my summer. Time to hermit."

Chapter 21

She only had a three-and-a-half-hour break between shifts, but Eden packed as much relaxing in as she could. A nice long bubble bath, homemade chocolate chip cookies, and she even managed a short nap. There were certainly more of those to come this summer! Plus, she put four more pieces into Maimoe's puzzle while waiting on cookies to bake.

While Eden relaxed, Ashley labored with the cash register. When Eden arrived at work, Ashley had a good enough handle on it to begin teaching Eden.

Eden was still struggling to understand how the complicated machine worked when the phone rang and Ashley answered. "This is The Pizza Parlor. Ashley speaking. How may I help you? Yes, just a minute."

Ashley handed the phone to Eden. "It's for you."

Eden gave her a quizzical look as she took the receiver. "This is Eden."

"Eden, this is Lucas."

"Lucas? Where are you?"

"I'm following Mrs. Emmet, like you asked. We're almost back to Halstead."

OMG! She felt awful. She had sent him to follow Mrs. Emmet and make sure she was okay, then forgot all about them. What kind of friend was she? What if Mrs. Emmet hadn't been okay, and Eden was eating a chocolate chip cookie in a relaxing hot bubble bath, fiddling the afternoon away?

"Lucas! You weren't supposed to leave town. What if Officer Dirks finds out?"

"Yeah, well, that's why I'm calling. Mickey called and asked me to stop by the police station. I was going to come by The Pizza Parlor and tell you Mrs. Emmet was okay, but Mickey needs to see me."

"Where have you been?"

"The casino."

"This whole time?"

"Yep. Mrs. Emmet drove straight there. I tried to go in but you have to be twenty-one, so I waited until she came out, then followed her back toward Halstead."

Eden bit her lower lip. "What do you think Mickey wants? Does he know you've been out of town?"

"Oh, I don't know. I don't think he does, but it's no big deal. I go by the police station all the time. Anyhow, just wanted to let you know Mrs. Emmet was fine. I gotta go."

When Eden looked up, she startled.

Mickey stood in the doorway waving for her to come over.

Ashley looked back at her with wide eyes, as if asking what Mickey wanted.

Eden nonchalantly shrugged her shoulders, but inside she was a ball of knots. This couldn't be anything good.

Mickey led her outside so they could talk privately. He whispered to the point he was hard to hear.

"I need your help."

Perplexed, Eden asked, "What's going on? Lucas just called and said you asked him to meet you at the police station."

"His fingerprints are all over the doctor's lab."

"So? My fingerprints are all over the lab too."

Officer Johnson nodded. "We know."

"Oh. Ohhh… But you don't think—"

"With the two of you spending time together snooping around, well, Officer Dirks is concerned you may be involved and using your investigation to cover up our suspicions."

Officer Johnson paused to scan the area before continuing. "Look, we already had reason to suspect Lucas was involved with Dr. Emmet's disappearance. Now his prints are all over the murder scene. I can't say why, but yes, we are investigating this as a murder. With the other evidence pointing toward Lucas, well, Officer Dirks is convinced Lucas had something to do with it. He'll hold Lucas a day or two while we try to locate a murder weapon. I know Lucas isn't perfect, and if I thought he was involved, I would arrest him myself. But I know he didn't kill anyone."

"But we didn't have a motive to kill the mayor," Eden protested.

"You don't, which keeps you at arm's length, for now. But Lucas does. You said yourself that the mayor gave him cash in order to keep quiet about the doctor's disappearance."

"How can you use my testimony to convict Lucas, then accuse me of being an accomplice?" Eden protested.

"Slow down," Officer Johnson said. "Obviously there's still a lot to sort through. I don't think either of you were involved with the mayor's murder, but there is substantial evidence that looks bad for the both of you."

"I thought you arrested Sam for the murder?"

"No, no. We tried to question him at his home but he was uncooperative and became physically agitated. We arrested him for his own safety. Other than his threat at city council, there's no evidence against him. He won't be held long."

"What can I do to help?"

"I don't believe your theory about the time machine, but in pursuing this case you've proven you're tenacious and a creative thinker. Keep thinking about the case and see if there's anything you can think of that will help me find out who really did this. That may be the only way we keep Lucas out of jail. And if he goes, you might not be far behind."

"Okay, I'll do what I can."

Eden drifted into The Pizza Parlor.

"What did Officer Johnson want?" Ashley asked anxiously.

She slowly met Ashley's eyes. "We're back on the case. I have something I need you to do."

Chapter 22

After work Eden went home, had dinner with Maimeo and played Yahtzee for an hour and a half. Once it turned dark she said good night, then laid in bed waiting for her grandma to go to sleep.

She dressed in a dark, long-sleeved shirt and jeans. She didn't want to be too obvious that she was sneaking around, but she wanted to blend in to the dark night.

She followed Ashley's directions to Jessica's house. It must have been a mile walk, all the way on the other side of town.

If nothing else, she might get in shape living in Halstead without a car. Maybe she would even lose a few of these extra ten pounds. Oh, who was she kidding? It was more like twenty or twenty-five.

Jessica's house was an average-sized, tan house in the middle of the block. She approached from the alley and when she got close, she could see a light on in a back room.

She crept up and peered in the back window, and her mouth dropped open. She would have been less surprised if she had been staring at an alien.

Mrs. Emmet rummaged through the drawers of a desk. When she opened the bottom right-hand drawer, she pulled out the book Eden had seen Jessica with earlier that morning. She was close enough to see the cover clearly: a painted picture of the time machine, with the initials *JB* scribbled in the bottom right-hand corner.

"That's the book that Jessica took from the hospital," Eden whispered to herself. "I've got to see what's in it."

Mrs. Emmet shut the drawer, locked it, and placed a small key in a false book cover and slid it into the bookshelf amidst dozens of other books.

Eden darted around the corner of the house, ducking out of sight just before Mrs. Emmet exited the back door. The older woman leaned over, her butt aimed toward Eden. What was she doing? Moments later she wandered into the alley and out of sight with Jessica's time machine book.

Chapter 23

*E*den had planned to get up early enough to visit Lucas in jail before work, but with her lack of sleep recently, she slept through her alarm. She had to run, again—ugh—to make it to work on time. She would go see him when her shift ended.

It was not meant to be. Since Ashley had figured out how to run the new cash register, Toby wanted her to teach Eden between the restaurant's lunch and dinner busy hours. Each hour that passed ate at her conscience for not visiting Lucas. She promised Mickey she would help and here she was, stuck at work and ignoring Lucas and the case.

Learning how to run the new cash register was a horribly slow, tedious, and agonizing process. Eden wanted to give up several times, but to her credit, Ashley patiently repeated instructions until finally, four hours later, Eden and Ashley agreed that Eden would run the register during the dinner rush.

Eden's feet ached after seven hours of standing with only a short lunch break. She hoped she could still visit Lucas after her dinner shift. She thought she should find Mickey and apologize to him for getting caught up at work.

Dinner time was busy but the time went fast. Eden took a deep breath when the line to order subsided. Her stiff fingers and rubbery legs ensured she would sleep well tonight. She shifted uncomfortably but could not release the pain throbbing in both knees.

The door dinged and she looked up. By now she thought surprises had run their course—a time machine, a dead body, Mrs. Emmet stealing from Jessica—but once again she was stunned. She ran to the front door and threw her arms around Lucas. Lucas appeared flustered.

It took Eden a moment to realize what she had just done, then she flushed and quickly let go, and tried quite unsuccessfully to play it cool.

"I thought you were in jail."

She blushed even more, realizing she'd just announced to The Pizza Parlor crowd she thought Lucas was in jail.

"I'm so sorry," she quickly whispered to Lucas. She grabbed his arm and pulled him toward the kitchen.

"I can't go back there."

"It's fine! I need to know what happened to you at the police station."

She tried to pull again but he was too strong for her to budge.

Then he chuckled.

"What's so funny?" Eden asked.

"I've been banned from here, remember?"

How could she have forgotten? Eden couldn't help herself and laughed with him. She motioned to Ashley, then stepped outside to talk to Lucas in private.

"I'm sorry. I meant to come visit you in jail, but they had me work all afternoon. How did you get out?"

"Well, they don't have a murder weapon so they couldn't keep me. Officer Dirks is going to search the hospital again for a weapon."

"But you didn't do it!" Eden protested.

"It doesn't matter at this point. My fingerprints are all over the crime scene and they know I had some shady dealings with the mayor."

"I'm sorry. They might not have connected you to the mayor's death had I not insisted you kidnapped Dr. Emmet. I'm going to get you out of it," Eden said.

"How?"

She contemplated. "I don't know. We need to figure out what really happened and who killed Mayor Washburn. The best clue we have, I think, is with the book that Mrs. Emmet took from Jessica. I think we should go to her house when I get off of work and ask her to let us look at it; see if there's anything useful in it."

"Do you think she'll let us look at it?"

"I'm sure she'll help. She knows I've been trying to figure out what happened to her husband. She's been helpful to me, and so nice. But I'll beg if I have to. I get off in thirty minutes. Meet me out back and we'll go visit Mrs. Emmet."

After work Lucas gave her a ride to Mrs. Emmet's.

As they approached her front door, Lucas said, "You don't think she's actually going to show us the book, do you?"

"She will if she doesn't want us to tell your cousin about it."

"Breaking and entering, now extortion. And I thought *I* was the troublemaker."

Eden knocked on Mrs. Emmet's door but she didn't answer. After pounding several times, she walked purposefully to the back of the house, and stopped short. One of the miniature, square window panes was broken, with small smears of blood dripping on the jagged edges. When Eden knocked on the back door, it creaked open.

Lucas looked as frightened as Eden felt. She swallowed and pushed the door open. "Mrs. Emmet? Are you in there?"

Eden put her foot in the doorframe, but Lucas placed his arm in front of her to hold her back.

"We're in enough trouble already."

"What if Mrs. Emmet's inside and injured? Or in danger?"

"Maybe we should call the police." Lucas padded his khaki pockets. "The police kept my phone so they can analyze my calls and texts. You're going to have to call."

"My phone's broken, remember?"

Lucas looked at her and she pleaded with her eyes for him to go in and make sure Mrs. Emmet was safe.

"I'll go first," he sighed.

For once she decided not to argue with him.

He stepped up onto the linoleum floor. Glass crunched underneath his large feet. Pieces of dried dirt were scattered on the floor of an otherwise clean and tidy laundry room. Something smelled burnt.

Eden hoped Mrs. Emmet was okay, but had a queasy feeling in the pit of her stomach.

Lucas picked up a broom and held it like he was stepping into the batter's box.

Eden grabbed the mop, mostly for the comfort of clutching something in her hands. She wouldn't be much help in a physical altercation.

Lucas entered the kitchen.

Eden stayed as close to him as she could without bumping him. Everything in the kitchen looked clean and in place except the teapot on the oven. That's where the burning smell was coming from! Eden rushed over and turned the stove off. She flipped through drawers until she found a pot holder and carefully set the pot in the sink.

After ensuring the pantry was empty of any bad guys or Mrs. Emmet's dead body, which Eden feared they would find, they searched the rest of the house. Thankfully, they were alone.

Lucas sat down in front of the computer.

"What are you doing?"

"This is an old computer but I think I can get it to work."

"What are you going to do? Update your Facebook status? Let's see: Current location, inside Mrs. Emmet's house. Maybe we can take some selfies by the back door and the blood on the floor so we can further incriminate ourselves. Shall I just call Mickey so we can turn ourselves in now?"

"Relax." He said it in such a laid-back manner Eden wanted to strangle him. If she thought she could pull it off…

"Wow." The wow was also drawn out to such a degree that Eden knew something had blown his mind. She had to admit that wouldn't take much.

"What is it?"

"Her history is full of online gambling sites."

"She's quite the gambler. So what?"

"She's not very good."

Lucas flew through web pages so quickly Eden couldn't follow. "How can you tell?"

He stopped on a page and pointed it out to her. "I'm looking at her account balances. There's a lot of up and downs, but she's adding money to these accounts on almost a weekly basis. I haven't seen a withdrawal yet."

"So she loses all the time? Why would she keep playing?"

"Oh, she has some big wins." He pointed out one where she had won nearly ten thousand dollars. "But she keeps playing with the winnings until they dwindle away. She never takes them out."

"How much has she lost?" Eden was now curious about Mrs. Emmet's gambling behavior.

"She's losing thousands of dollars a week. And that's going back several months."

"What else can you tell?"

"She left her e-mail open." Lucas scrolled through several dozen e-mails. "Most of these look like advertisements for the gambling sites. She needs to clean out the spam."

"Wait!" Eden grabbed Lucas's shoulder as if she could control his actions by doing so. If she just had one muscle in her body as strong as his shoulder. She quickly let go, thankful he faced the computer and was unable to see her blush.

She pointed to the screen. "Who's Boris Yugov?"

Lucas opened the e-mail and read.

"We have been most worried since your husband disappeared. Gaylord has not been helpful, though he insists he still wants to sell. My client will not accept an outcome other than his purchase of the machine."

Mrs. Emmet had replied:

"We don't need Roger and Gaylord. I want to make the deal as quickly as possible. When can we talk?"

Lucas scrolled up and read the last response from Boris.

"*We'll be in touch. If this deal falls through I assure you someone will pay.*"

"Holy cow!" Lucas exclaimed. "Do you think the Russians killed the mayor?"

"No, look at the date. These e-mails were written early this morning."

"What do you think they mean?" Lucas asked, rising from the chair.

Eden paced. "Mayor Washburn and Dr. Emmet were going to sell the time machine to the Russians, but now Mrs. Emmet wants to sell it? Let me think a minute."

She wandered through the dining room, through the entryway, and into the parlor.

The room had a faint odor of smoke. The magazines on the coffee table—Reader's Digest, AARP, and Travel & Leisure—were scattered and not in the nice, neat stacks they had been before.

Eden started to pass by them when she noticed something glimmer. She picked up the Good House-keeping magazine, and a cigarette lighter fell to the floor. This wasn't just any lighter; it was an *Absolut Vodka* lighter.

What was Sam's lighter doing here?

She ran out the back door, Lucas right on her tail, and threw open the door to the detached garage. Parked where it should be was the green Cadillac.

"I guess she didn't go to the casino," Lucas observed.

Eden slammed the door and started walking down the alley. "Call Mickey and tell him someone broke into Mrs. Emmet's house."

Lucas shouted, "Where are we going?"

"To see Sam Nelson."

Chapter 24

Lucas borrowed his sister's phone and notified Officer Johnson of what they had found at Mrs. Emmet's. By the time they arrived at Sam Nelson's house the sun was gone. Light shone out the front window through Sam's tattered blinds. A silhouette moved across the blinds. At least he hadn't passed out yet.She knocked on the door, grateful to have Lucas by her side. As much as he annoyed her, Lucas was turning out to be useful—comforting, even.

Sam jerked the door open. "What do you want?"

She recognized the voice and attitude, but not the look. Over his usual tank top t-shirt he wore an open short-sleeve, button-down shirt. His jeans were clean, his face clean-shaven, and his dark hair combed straight back. The smell of alcohol fled his home like an escaping convict, but he smelled strongly like after-shave.

"What do you want?" Sam barked again.

Their last meeting—his breath; his touch; his threat—flooded back into her mind. She thought she might vomit all over him. She quickly choked back the nauseating feeling. "I, uh… we, um… we have a question about the doctor."

"Yeah? What about him?" Sam held the door and didn't move to invite them in or step out to converse with them. Why would he be hospitable after he caught her with his book?

Should she come right out and accuse him of doing something to Mrs. Emmet? She wanted to. But she thought better of that idea since she had left the lighter at Mrs. Emmet's house so the police could find it as evidence. "Did you ever overhear anything about a time machine and the Russians?"

"Time machine? What are you talking about, girl?"

Lucas chuckled and Eden elbowed him. "I believe the machine Dr. Emmet built in the hospital is a time machine and that he and Mayor Washburn and Jessica Barns were trying to sell it to the Russians. Do you know anything about it?"

Sam gave a long, admiring whistle. "You sure do have quite an imagination."

"Surely you overheard something," she pressed.

"Didn't you read about it when you stole my journal?" he said bitterly.

"I-I…" Eden's anger rose, but then she reminded herself that she was the one at fault. "I'm sorry. It was wrong of me to take and read your journal. I don't think I read near as much as you think I did, though."

Her apology seemed to catch him off guard. He stared down for a long moment. When he looked back up, he didn't address her apology, but it seemed to have the desired effect.

His tone softened. "Most of the time I didn't get close enough to hear them talk. I did hear those two quack doctors arguing one time in Dr. Emmet's house. I was outside and only caught part of what they said, but the gist of the argument was whether they should sell the invention, as they called it, to the Russians."

"When was this?" Lucas asked.

"A couple of weeks ago, maybe less."

"You said, 'those *two* doctors?' So Mayor Washburn was a doctor too."

"Of course he was. Now, are we through here?"

"Sure," Eden managed to get out before the door slammed.

"I thought you were going to ask him about the lighter," Lucas asked quizzically.

Eden turned and followed the sidewalk away from Sam's house. "I didn't have proof and he would have just denied it."

"Then why did we come?" Lucas demanded.

"He gave us confirmation about the Russians wanting to buy the time machine, didn't he?"

"Yeah, but so what? We already knew that."

"We didn't know the doctor and mayor disagreed." Eden found a large oak tree across the street and stood with it between her and Sam's house. "Besides, we need proof he did something to Mrs. Emmet."

Lucas crossed his arms, staring at her. "How is that going to help me stay out of jail?"

"I don't know," she admitted. She grabbed his arm and pulled him toward her. "Now stay out of sight or Sam will know we are watching."

Lucas seemed put out; probably not used to being manhandled by a girl. "What makes you think we're going to see anything?"

"He had showered and shaved. I doubt he does that to hang out in his house."

Shortly, Sam came around the side of his house carrying a shovel and a lantern. He opened the trunk and tossed them in, on top of a blanket that covered a nearly full trunk.

Eden gawked. The quilt! A quilt with purple daisies. It wasn't just any quilt—it was Mrs. Emmet's!

Sam slammed it shut and drove away.

"Was that Mrs. Emmet in his trunk?" Lucas asked.

"It was her blanket, and it was covered with blood. We have to follow him!"

They hurried to Lucas's car and carefully trailed Sam. He drove two miles north of town and turned onto a dirt road and under an archway that read, *Halstead Cemetery*. Lucas drove past, turned off his lights and parked on a nearby gravel road. Sam smoked a cigarette and drank a beer while sitting on his trunk. He tossed the butt and covered his face with his hands. He wept so hard his whole body convulsed. Then he wiped his tears on his shirt sleeve and lit another cigarette. He continued this cycle for thirty minutes before he drove off.

Lucas pulled around to where Sam had been and Eden hopped out. The gravestone said *Samuel Luke Nelson, 07-02-92 to 05-15-21.*

"It was his son," Eden told Lucas when she got back into the car. "Monday was the twentieth anniversary of his son's death."

Lucas quickly caught up to trailing distance of Sam and followed him fifteen miles to the Harvey County West Park campgrounds. Sam passed the crowded campground area and drove around to the far side of the lake. Lucas turned his headlights out as soon as they exited the campground area so Sam wouldn't notice him following. Sam parked and Lucas pulled off the road and into a tree grove to hide the car. He and Eden got out and hid behind trees where they could discreetly watch Sam from a distance.

Sam set his lantern on a flat rock, then set up his tent and built a fire. He opened his trunk and retrieved the shovel. He dug a hole as he sipped on his third beer since arriving.

"What are we going to do?" Lucas asked in a panic.

Eden wiped away a tear. She'd liked Mrs. Emmet. "We have to call the police," Eden said. "Call Mickey and tell him we're watching Sam Nelson bury Mrs. Emmet."

Lucas pulled his sister's phone from his pocket. "I don't have any reception."

"We have to find somewhere with a signal."

"I'll go," Lucas volunteered. "You can keep an eye on Sam."

Eden gritted her teeth. "There's no way you're leaving me in the middle of nowhere with a killer and a dead body."

They backtracked to the campgrounds but still no signal. Lucas continued to drive south until they reached Highway 50.

"Give me your phone. I'll call since you're driving."

Lucas fished the phone from his pocket and handed it to Eden. "He's number five on speed dial."

"But this isn't your phone."

"He's number five on all of our speed dials."

She pressed five.

"Lucas? I've been searching for you. Where are you?"

"This is Eden. Lucas is driving. We followed Sam Nelson out to, to... where are we again?" she asked Lucas.

"Harvey County West."

"To Harvey County West Lake. He's digging a hole to bury Mrs. Emmet."

"What? Is this some kind of joke?"

"No joke!"

"Let me talk to Lucas."

Eden handed the phone to Lucas. "Yes. Yes. No, she's telling the truth. We saw Mrs. Emmet wrapped in a blanket in his trunk. He's digging a big hole now. He's going to bury her for sure."

Lucas gave Mickey directions to Sam's campsite and hung up. "He's on his way. He said to wait for him at the campgrounds and not to go back to watch Sam."

"Like that's going to happen," Eden said sarcastically.

When they returned, Sam was shoveling dirt back into the hole, the blanket was spread across the top of the car, and the trunk was empty. Within minutes, Mickey drove up with red and blue lights illuminating the campsite.

The unexpected company didn't seem to phase Sam one bit. He leaned the shovel against the car and picked up his beer. He lit a cigarette as Officer Dirks and Mickey approached. Both officers had hands on their holsters. Eden and Lucas stayed out of sight.

"We had a report you might be out here burying a body," Officer Dirks said as he and Mickey stopped twenty feet from Sam, who seemed as relaxed as if they were shooting the breeze at a church picnic.

"That's right."

"Where did you bury her?"

Sam flipped his head toward the burial site. "Over there."

Officer Dirks nodded to Mickey, who picked up the shovel and started digging up the hole Sam had just finished filling.

"Who did you bury?" Officer Dirks asked.

"Mrs. Thomas." Sam gave him a wry smile.

"Who's Mrs. Thomas?"

"My cat."

They waited in silence as Mickey dug. Finally he returned to confirm Sam's claim.

"Are you through desecrating Mrs. Thomas's grave?" Sam was smugger than usual.

Officer Dirks nodded. "Sorry for the inconvenience, Sam. But when we get a tip we have to follow it up. We'll be glad to refill the hole."

"Don't bother." Sam waved him off. "I'll finish it. I just want some peace and quiet."

As the two officers returned to their car, Sam yelled at them, "You can tell your cousin and his girlfriend I know they called in the tip." He laughed a deep, disturbing laugh.

Chapter 25

"Do you realize the danger you put yourselves in by following Sam instead of notifying us immediately? What if he *did* have a body in his trunk? You guys could have been next!" The questions were rhetorical; Eden learned that thirty minutes ago when she answered the first question Officer Dirks had asked. His face and ears were bright red and Eden was thankful for the table between them.

She was too afraid to look away from him.

Lucas constantly fidgeted with his hands and stared at the floor. It would get worse for him once Mickey and his family took their turn. And for her once her probation officer heard.

Finally Officer Dirks's tone softened and his voice quieted down to a normal, indoor speaking volume. "I know you think you are doing the right thing, but trust me, we have a handle on the murder case and don't need any further help.

"And as for Mrs. Emmet, we're looking into it. So far there's no evidence she was home when the break-in occurred. Honestly, at this point you two are our most likely suspects for breaking into her house."

"But we didn't—" Eden started, but he put up his hand for her not to speak.

Officer Dirks stood and leaned against the back of his chair. "Mickey took your statements last night and we will continue to investigate. Don't think you're out of the woods on this. I would lock you up until these cases are solved, but I think it could be a while and I can't legally hold you more than a few hours without charging you with a crime." He shifted his arms from the chair to the table, so he leaned close to Eden's face. "And you can't afford another arrest—guilty or not—can you?"

Eden swallowed hard. Of course! He had checked into her back-ground and knew all about her probation. Any kind of trouble in Halstead would probably get her in serious hot water with her probation officer. She couldn't afford that.

She nodded. Officer Dirks relaxed and placed his hand on the doorknob, as if to leave.

But Mrs. Emmet... "If Sam didn't take Mrs. Emmet, what about the Russians?" Eden protested.

"Technically we don't know that anyone took Mrs. Emmet."

Eden was crestfallen.

"We have a Forensic Computer Specialist coming this afternoon to look at Mrs. Emmet's computer. She'll find anything that's on the computer, you needn't worry about that."

"This afternoon?" Eden exploded. "What if Mrs. Emmet is trying to sell the time machine to the Russians? She could be in real danger!"

"Please, Miss Price. Let it go. We'll get to the bottom of this. You two go be teenagers and stop interfering." He leaned across the desk and looked Eden straight in the eyes. "I'd hate to arrest you for obstruction of justice. Can you give me your word you'll stay away from this case?"

Eden's determination faded. "Yes, sir."

"Good." Officer Dirks opened the door. "You're free to go for now. But remain available until we make an arrest in the murder case. And we may still have more questions about Mrs. Emmet."

Chapter 26

Normally Eden would have been excited to be turned loose on her own at the front counter.

It meant not having to make pizzas, after all. But her heart wasn't in it after the chewing out she had received from Officer Dirks. She went through the motions of greeting customers and ringing up orders, but after the lunch crowd began to slow, she realized she didn't remember much about what had happened during the previous hour.

Ashley popped out of the office, the first time Eden had seen her since she arrived at work.

"What are you doing back there?"

"Well, remember how I told you the owner likes to go overboard on his purchases?"

Eden nodded.

"He bought a new copier. I guess it's 'super speedy'," she laughed. "Whatever that means. Now he's volunteering to run flyers for everybody. It's the first time that both our baseball and softball teams have been to the state tournament, so I'm working on flyers. Then we'll make copies so the teams can hand them out door-to-door, inviting everyone to a big parade and pep rally, and a send-off next week."

"What do you think?" Ashley handed her a proto-type flyer, colored with the dragon (the school's mascot) blue, green grass, and baby blue sky. The parade and bonfire were scheduled for next Tuesday evening, then the send-off Wednesday afternoon as both teams would leave for their respective tournament sites.

"It looks great! But won't that be expensive?"

"We'll only run a few in color to hang up in the stores. The rest will be black and white."

Eden quickly told her about her and Lucas falsely accusing Sam of killing Mrs. Emmet, but before Ashley could respond, more customers came in, so Ashley retreated back to the office.

Eden tried to put the case out of her mind, but the lack of answers nagged at her. She worried about Mrs. Emmet, and Dr. Emmet. She hated the thought, but she worried about what might happen to her if Mrs. Emmet didn't return or was fatally hurt. Could she truly be a suspect? Lucas had been right. They should have called the police when they found Mrs. Emmet's house broken into.

Everything she had touched failed. Now she had been banned from the case. She wanted to be done with it, true, but on her own terms.

"Excuse me?" A customer stood on the other side of the counter and she hadn't noticed.

"May I help you?"

Before the lady could order, Eden looked at the monitor on the cash register and gave a shriek.

Ashley came quickly from the office. "What's the matter?"

Eden stood, frozen, staring at the register. She pointed at the blank monitor. "I think I broke it. All the numbers disappeared. What did I do?"

Ashley tried, unsuccessfully, to stifle a laugh. Eden glared at her, still frightened, and confused at why Ashley would laugh when she had damaged the new cash register. Ashley pressed the keyboard and the screen popped back to life. That's when Eden realized what had happened.

"It's fine. The screen just went to sleep," Ashley explained.

"I didn't realize it was like a computer," Eden said as she blushed. The lady waiting to order probably thought she was an idiot.

Chapter 27

"What's wrong?" Her grandmother's voice startled her.

She hadn't heard her enter the kitchen; or the house, now that she thought about it. "Nothing."

Maimeo gave her that I-know-you're-not-telling-me-the-truth scowl. "You've been staring at that puzzle for ten minutes and haven't moved a single piece."

Eden didn't dare tell her everything, but she knew she had to give her something. "I'm still worried about Mrs. Emmet." She said it while working on the puzzle so Maimeo couldn't see her face and realize she was holding back. The fiasco at the lake the previous night had caused Eden to be late, so she had explained how she and Lucas had stopped to check on Mrs. Emmet and found her back door ajar and they were out looking for her and lost track of time.

Maimeo joined her puzzle work. "I'm sure the police are doing everything they can to find her."

They were, but they didn't believe Eden about the time machine so they could be looking in the wrong places.

"An investigation is a lot like working a puzzle. You gather all the pieces, sort through them, but not until you place each piece into the correct place does the big picture make sense."

Eden chuckled. "You sure do like your puzzle metaphors, don't you?"

Maimeo smiled and nodded.

"What happens if the police don't find all of the pieces and they can't tell what the puzzle looks like?"

"You have to think positive, Peaches. I'm sure Mrs. Emmet will turn up soon." Maimeo held Eden's hand and smiled for a moment before standing. "Now, I must go to my book club. Are you okay with leftovers? There are some in the fridge you can warm up for dinner."

Maimeo left, but Eden still couldn't relax. She found herself constantly looking out the back windows, then the front, then the back again, to see if Lucas had returned home. He never showed. She tried to eat, to read, to nap, to eat some more, but nothing settled her. At one point Eden got so desperate to escape the monotony, she went for a walk, but the ninety degrees chased her home after only four blocks.

Eden sat in the glider on the back porch, placed a Pringle into her mouth, then another, then another. The last time Eden sat in this chair, Sam had paid an unwelcome visit. She shuddered at the thought, then shifted uncomfortably. She had the night off of work. It was going to be a long evening.

Her grandmother's home phone rang and she jumped. She followed the rings into the kitchen and found the phone in a corner beside the bread box. "Hello?"

"Eden?"

"Who is this?"

"This is Mrs. Emmet." Her voice was quiet, desperate.

Eden's was not. "Mrs. Emmet. Are you okay?"

"I've been trying to call your cell phone but it kept going to voice mail."

"I'm sorry. My cell phone broke." Eden paced, but quickly had the long cord that connected the handset to the telephone wrapped around her body.

"Please, dear, I need your help."

"Sure, anything." Eden spun in circles to untangle herself from the coil cord.

"I need you and Lucas to meet me in Roger's lab. Say nine o'clock?"

"I'm not allowed in the hospital—Jessica's orders."

"I'm desperate, Eden, and I don't know who I can trust. No one can know you're coming, and don't park that boy's car anywhere near the hospital or my house."

Eden hesitated. How much trouble was Mrs. Emmet in? "Okay. I'll get Lucas and Mickey."

"No!" Mrs. Emmet's voice had momentarily lost its whisper, but she quickly recovered. "No police. It's too dangerous."

Eden was horrified. "Are you sure you're okay? You sound like you're in trouble. I know Mickey would do anything he—"

"No, dear. I'm sorry, but I can't risk it. I'll explain when you get here. Please trust me."

"I haven't seen Lucas since this morning but I'll try to find him."

"Thank you." Mrs. Emmet's voice relaxed for the first time during the phone call. "I'll see you at nine."

Eden glanced at the kitchen clock. Five forty-eight. What could she do to help? Think!

Surely if the Russians had Mrs. Emmet she wouldn't have been able to call. But who, then, was Mrs. Emmet worried about? Sam? Maybe, but Eden didn't think so. Jessica? Well, Jessica gave Eden the creeps, and seemed her most likely suspect. That's where she should start.

Without her cell phone she didn't know Lucas's phone number. She ran to his house and knocked on the door, but no one answered. She would have to proceed without him.

She walked by the hospital to confirm Jessica's SUV was there, then continued on to her house. She walked through the alley, into Jessica's back yard, and stopped by the back door where she had seen Mrs. Emmet bend over after stealing the book from Jessica's house. She leaned beside the bush and examined the hundreds of smooth, light-colored rocks. She noticed one bigger rock against the house with a dark brown tone. She picked it up, shook it, and something rattled inside, so she twisted the rock and it popped open. A key fell to the ground; the key Mrs. Emmet had used to enter the house and steal the book.

How would Mrs. Emmet know where Jessica hid a key? She understood why Mrs. Emmet would want some answers, but she didn't take her for the type who would break into someone's house. Then again, she'd known the location of the key, so maybe she and Jessica were friends and it hadn't been breaking in. But Mrs. Emmet had taken Jessica's book, so it was at least stealing. Eden's mind went in circles.

Inside, the long, back room housed a washer and dryer to Eden's right, and a makeshift office to her left. She squeezed between the rolling chair tucked neatly under the desk and a tall, stand-alone file cabinet against the back wall. She scanned the bookshelf full of books on business management and self-discipline, until she found the fake book where Mrs. Emmet had replaced the desk drawer key.

Eden took the key to the desk and quickly opened a drawer, sifted through the contents, then slammed it shut and moved to the next. Eden hoped to find a clue to Mrs. Emmet's relationship with Jessica, but nothing stood out to her. She opened the bottom left drawer and stopped.

On top was a brochure. She opened it and saw a beautiful, lush island. At first Eden thought it was a travel brochure, but across the top it read, "This could be yours for under $10 million.' An aerial view of the island gave Eden a sense of the size. She thought her high school might fit on the island. Maybe.

A sticky note with a handwritten message said, *'Another $23 million and we can build our dream house and buy a yacht for travel. G.'*

Was that G— as in Gaylord? Eden wondered. But Ashley had told her the mayor was going broke. How could he, or they, afford their own island? Unless they were expecting a financial windfall.

"Why am I not surprised to find you here, Price?"

Eden spun, her heart racing. Crap! Jessica stood between her and the door. She scolded herself for not paying attention.

"Return to the scene of the crime? Gaylord's journal wasn't enough for you?"

"I-I didn't take the journal."

If she thought Eden had taken it, then she didn't know the real culprit. But that didn't matter now. Eden was busted, caught red-handed. She would get her turn to ride in a police car. Her probation officer would be contacted. She might not see daylight again for a while.

"I'm sorry. I thought you were at the hospital and—"

"And me being at work gives you permission to break into my house? My neighbor called to inform me someone was suspiciously snooping around in my back yard."

"I didn't break in. Honest."

She folder her arms. "Yet here we are, inside my house. You, without my permission."

Eden dropped her head. "I didn't break in; I found your hidden key outside. I'm trying to find out who killed the mayor. I thought it might be you, but, but now I don't think so."

Jessica glared, her face red with rage, for an uncomfortably long time—so long that Eden wanted to call Mickey herself just to keep Jessica from doing something worse. Jessica's eyes dropped to the brochure Eden still held, and her demeanor immediately changed. She slowly reached out and took the brochure from Eden as if it were breakable. She mumbled something and stepped to the side, her eyes moist; her gaze glued to the brochure.

"Excuse me?"

"Get out!"

She's letting me go? Eden watched her, afraid to leave and afraid to stay. Jessica paid her no attention as she disappeared into the next room with tears falling onto the brochure. Eden placed the key on the desk and ran all the way home.

Chapter 28

*E*den had only been home a few minutes when a loud bang on the back door shook her nerves. She hurried from her room to find Lucas pounding away. He wore a white shirt with three-quarter blue sleeves, baseball pants, and his 'H' cap. The knees and sides of the pants were covered with dirt. The shirt and face were covered with dirt mixed with sweat. He smelled as bad as he looked. Instead of inviting his filthiness in, she stepped outside.

"Let me guess, baseball practice?"

"Only a few more days until the state tournament." Lucas smiled proudly. She told him all about Mrs. Emmet's call and her strange run-in with Jessica.

"That's why I came by. You don't have to worry about Jessica anymore. She's been arrested for Mayor Washburn's murder."

"What?" Earlier Eden had been convinced Jessica kidnapped Mrs. Emmet. How come Jessica's arrest surprised her?

"Mickey and Officer Dirks found the murder weapon in Jessica's office. A syringe."

So that's how he died. She couldn't explain it, but Jessica's arrest didn't feel right, so she talked Lucas into going to the hospital early to have a look at Jessica's office. Around eight-thirty, after Lucas had showered and changed, they parked his car at the high school and hoofed the three blocks to the hospital.

Lucas popped open the back door of the hospital then scooped up the gray kitten. "Hello Velma."

"Velma? You named the cat after a cartoon character?"

"Kitten. And of course. Velma's the one who discovered Mayor Washburn's dead body so I named her after the greatest female detective."

"I'm not calling her Velma."

They exited the cafeteria and walked the hallway.

"Why do you hate Velma?"

"I don't hate the kitten. I just, it's just, think about it. V—, she lives by eating mice and rats and stuff. And then you snuggle with her and let her lick you." Eden cringed. "That's just gross."

Lucas covered Velma's ears. "Don't listen to the mean girl. She's just jealous because you're a better detective than she is.

Eden almost laughed out loud. Almost.

"What do you hope to find?" he asked as they approached Jessica's office.

"I'm not sure. A clue." Eden flipped the lights on.

Lucas set Velma down and she immediately hopped onto Jessica's chair and up to the desk. Jessica's desk was clear. The boxes, her computer—all gone.

"So you don't think Jessica killed Mayor Washburn?"

"I don't know." She scanned through Jessica's top drawer while shooing Velma away and found office supplies—pencils, pens, paperclips, and rubber bands. In other words, nothing.

Lucas held up the keyboard from the back counter. "Why didn't they take these?"

She dug into the bottom drawer. Medical supplies, syringes, tongue depressors—all items sealed in their original packaging and no longer needed at the vacated hospital. Eden looked up at the keyboard Lucas held and the monitor sitting alone on the counter. "Why would they? You can't do anything with just a monitor and keyboard."

He set the keyboard down and hit some keys. The screen came to life. A grid of six squared pictures lined the monitor. Now he had her attention.

"How did you do that? It isn't plugged in or connected to anything. There are no wires."

"Have you ever heard of batteries and wireless connections?"

She hadn't even considered it. Obviously, neither had the police.

The boxes on the screen contained views from video cameras. Three were from outside the hospital, one of the main lobby, and one showed the hallway outside of Jessica's office. But Eden's eyes focused on the sixth picture—Dr. Emmet's lab and the time machine. The dark, empty room gave Eden the chills. In her mind, she watched the murder play out, different characters playing the leading part. But which one of them had played the true lead role?

Then it hit her. "If Jessica has a surveillance system, she'll have it recorded somewhere, right?"

"Yeah," Lucas agreed. "It probably feeds to a hard drive."

"Which would contain past video feeds?"

"It should. And if it goes back far enough, we might be able to see who killed the mayor!"

"But why didn't the police find it? Or did they?"

Lucas shook his head. "I don't think so. At least, Mickey didn't mention it…"

Eden ripped through the rest of the drawers. She found files with invoices and hospital records and other boring stuff. Then she searched the counter doors. It had to be here somewhere. She recklessly tossed out everything inside the cabinets—a box of cleaning supplies, tangled cords and wires, several mugs, a stack of t-shirts.

With the cabinets empty, she plopped herself down on the floor, dejected. Lucas sat beside her and together they stared into the emptiness below the counter. Velma nestled between them. What had she missed? Lucas sprang to his feet so fast that Velma jumped onto

Eden's lap and she instinctively turned away to protect the kitten.

He didn't seem to notice. "The counter isn't secured."

"What does that mean?" Eden stood, realized she was petting Velma, and quickly set her down.

"It means it isn't attached to the wall."

She didn't understand the significance until he scooted the counter away from the wall. He beamed. Several thin black boxes made it look like a miniature IT room.

"Why hide all of this?" Eden pondered.

"Unless you're doing something sinister."

Eden agreed. But this should also provide the police with proof of who killed Mayor Washburn.

Lucas pointed to the monitor. "Mrs. Emmet is in the doctor's lab."

The older woman was pacing, looking nervous.

Eden felt a pang of guilt for forgetting about Mrs. Emmet in the excitement of finding the hidden surveillance system. She quickly started for the door.

Lucas hesitated. "Shouldn't we clean up or something?"

"We need to help Mrs. Emmet. Then we'll call the police and show them what we found."

"But…but… "

"Is this about ghosts?"

"Maybe," he admitted.

"I promise, no ghosts."

He followed her, reluctantly.

When they arrived at the doctor's lab, Eden would have rather seen a ghost. Motioning them into the room was Mrs. Emmet, waving a gun.

Chapter 29

*E*den shrieked and grabbed Lucas's arm. Tight.

"Hands in the air where I can see them," Mrs. Emmet barked.

They obeyed. Mrs. Emmet tossed a pair of handcuffs to Lucas. "Handcuff yourself to the time machine."

Lucas looked at Eden as if asking her permission. What was she supposed to tell him to do? Don't obey the mad lady with a gun pointed at him?

"It's going to be okay," she tried to assure him, then turned to Mrs. Emmet. "What about me?"

"I have a special assignment for you."

"Why are you doing this?" Eden asked. "I mean, you asked me to trust you."

Eden thought she saw a moment of sadness on Mrs. Emmet's face, but the lady quickly steeled herself. "I told you, I'm in a lot of trouble and I need your help to get out of it."

"By pointing a gun at me?"

"I need you to do me a favor."

"I would have gladly done anything for you before. But not now."

"You might have. But you also may have gone to the police. Right now, I can't have them involved."

Eden shifted nervously. What did Mrs. Emmet have planned?

"But the police can protect you from the Russians."

"I'm not afraid of the Russians, dear. I don't want the police to know this is a time machine."

"Know? I didn't think you even believed it was a time machine."

"Gaylord's journal convinced me otherwise. And he was about to make a bundle of money, which I intend to make for myself."

"We thought you were in trouble. Someone broke into your house."

"Yes, Boris sent someone for me. After what happened to Roger and Gaylord, he feared losing out on the time machine. I told him I would secure the sale. Which brings me to you. I can't go to my house because the police have a computer tech and extra men present. Gaylord's journal is hidden inside the house and I can't have it being discovered."

"So you want me to get the journal for you?"

"Precisely, dear. And you'll have to be careful not to let anyone see you. If the police find out, I would hate to see what happens to your friend here."

Eden looked into Lucas's desperate eyes. "We're not exactly friends."

"So you're okay if I knock him off?"

Eden tried to keep up a brave face, but she couldn't let Lucas die. "I guess I don't hate him that much."

"Good." Mrs. Emmet explained where the journal was hidden and gave Eden a key to her house. "Now get going. We may not have much time."

The last thing Eden had expected to do this summer was try to save Lucas's life. As an officer she didn't recognize rounded the corner and walked down the side yard of the Emmet's house, Eden contemplated telling him the whole story. Would Mrs. Emmet really kill Lucas? In the end, she decided she couldn't take that chance. She had to get the journal and return it to Mrs. Emmet. After all, it was the *right* thing to do. Isn't that what Ashley would tell her?

She snuck up the porch and peered in the front window. No one. She used the key Mrs. Emmet had given her to quietly enter the house. She immediately froze. She heard Mickey's voice and almost ran to him, before her mind kicked in and reminded her of the consequences of getting the police involved. She heard a female voice speaking to Mickey and keystrokes pounding at a rapid rate. It must be the technician looking into Mrs. Emmet's computer. It wouldn't be long before the police knew of her gambling addiction and desire to sell the time machine. She had to hurry. Would those emails be enough to convince them the time machine was real? She didn't know but didn't have time to figure it out.

She crept through the parlor to the stairs, and quickly up. Locating the mayor's journal underneath a loose plank in the spare bedroom and securing it in the back of her jeans was easy; Mrs. Emmet had directed Eden to its special hiding place, after all. Getting back out of the house proved to be otherwise.

As Eden began down the stairway she saw a shadow near the bottom. The shadow lingered as she heard Mickey's voice, sounding almost flirty. She tenderly retraced her steps up and stood in the hallway, contemplating what to do next.

Suddenly footsteps bounded up the stairs and Eden darted her head around, undecided on what to do. She scampered into Mrs. Emmet's bedroom and scurried under the bed. Her heart pounded and she did her best to quiet her gasps for breath.

She saw dark shoes and the bottom of dark blue pants she assumed belonged to Mickey walk past the door. She breathed a sigh of relief too soon. He reversed course in the hall and entered the bedroom. From underneath the bed she watched Mickey's feet quickly make their way through the bedroom and into the master bathroom.

The sound of the toilet lid being raised, a zipper, then urine flowing into the toilet made Eden gasp in amazement. The door to the bathroom remained wide open. What was he thinking?

The toilet flushed, the light went dark, and Eden saw Mickey's feet roam the room once more, this time much slower than the first. He opened the closet door, turned on the light, then turned it out a few seconds later. Mickey's feet shuffled from the closet to the bed and stopped less than a foot from Eden's face.

Instinctively she held her breath and prayed. For a long, agonizing minute, she waited. At first she hoped he wouldn't find her, but by the time she couldn't hold in her breath any longer she wanted to be caught. Could he save Lucas if she told him everything?

The seconds ticked away. Surely he knew she was there. Why else would he just stand there for so long? Was he toying with her?

Just before she exhaled, Mickey left the room, making his way back downstairs. She crawled from underneath the bed and sat for a few minutes, gathering her wits about her. She couldn't escape the way she'd come in.

With her nerves gathered up, she raised the window and eyed the large oak tree towering in the back yard. With the mayor's journal snuggled tightly underneath her jeans, she carefully made her way down.

Chapter 30

When Eden returned to Dr. Emmet's lab she met a dejected Lucas petting Velma who laid across his lap without a care in the world. If Velma was so smart she would cozy up to the one with the gun instead of risking becoming collateral damage.

Seeing Lucas sitting on the floor, with his back to the wall and his handcuffed arm raised above his head, she felt something she had never experienced toward him—pity.

He stood excitedly on seeing her. Velma ran to Eden and rubbed up against her leg. Eden shook her head and placed the book on top of the monitor then approached Lucas. "Are you okay?"

"I'm fine." He shook his arm that he had held above him for who knows how long.

Mrs. Emmet stepped into the room from the attached office. "Do you have the book?"

Eden pointed.

The older woman quickly flipped the pages of the book to confirm she indeed had what she wanted, then tossed Eden a key. "Unchain him from the machine and handcuff yourselves together."

"I thought you were going to let us go," Lucas protested as Eden followed instructions.

"Pft! I can't very well let you go while I'm still in town, now can I?"

"What are you going to do?"

Eden didn't blame Lucas for his fear this time.

Mrs. Emmet typed on the keyboard. "I'm going to send you into the future—let's say three months. That way you can't interfere any more until after I am filthy rich and long gone. When you return, you can snoop around all you want; it won't matter." She paused, her face looking momentarily sad. "I'm sorry, dear. I wish you hadn't gotten all mixed up in this. I really do like you."

"Wait! I can't miss three months. We leave for the state tournament on Wednesday."

"So *now* you believe it's a time machine?" Eden demanded.

"I'm not sure. But you two keep talking like it is, and it's making me uneasy."

Velma stood on her back legs and pawed at Eden and then Lucas, who picked her up with his free arm. As Lucas petted the kitten, she pawed toward Eden, so Lucas shifted her to his handcuffed arm, allowing Velma easier access to Eden. She patted the kitten's head.

She didn't like the feline but sympathized with its nervousness. Lucas may or may not believe it's a time machine, but Eden knew better. She had glanced through Mayor Washburn's journal and seen the proof. Her eyes searched the room as her mind raced for an idea to keep her and Lucas out of the time machine.

Should she be concerned about survival? If Dr. Emmet had invented the machine and been willing to travel through time himself, surely she and Lucas would be fine, right? But what if Dr. Emmet hadn't traveled in time by choice? What if Mrs. Emmet put him there in order to get her hands on the machine? Or Mayor Washburn? Or someone else? According to the mayor's journal there had been some tragic mishaps early on while testing the machine. How safe was it now? She didn't know! She hadn't time to read the whole damn journal! Now that she faced the reality of being thrust into it, she doubted. She not only doubted, she struggled to believe it worked at all!

And then there was the issue of when they would return. If Mrs. Emmet had never run the time machine, what if she made a mistake? What if everyone Eden knew was gone when they returned? What if it was years or even decades from now? What if they couldn't return? If the Russians took the time machine it would mean disconnecting it from power. What would that mean for her and Lucas? Could they return, even if the Russians reconnected power before their scheduled return date?

Eden's heart raced. Her mind raced. She didn't trust Lucas to come up with a brilliant way out, but no good plan came to her, so she did one thing she had wanted to do since she'd met Lucas: she punched his arm as hard as she could.

"Ow! What was that for?"

"I had to hit something and I can't reach her."

"Don't do that again."

"Would you rather me hit Velma?"

She hadn't meant it, of course, and the shock on his face surprised her. He believed she would.

He took Velma in his free arm and held her away from Eden. "No, hit me."

She could tell he meant it and his sincerity choked her. She almost couldn't go through with it but closed her eyes and thought back to their first meeting. She punched him again.

His glare burned through Eden and she was glad Velma occupied his free hand.

"You got us into this mess! Now we're going to die!"

Her words seared. Lucas looked genuinely hurt. She would explain later. She shoved him and he stumbled. His flailing arm whipped Eden toward Mrs. Emmet. Eden swung her free arm and the gun went sprawling onto the floor. Mrs. Emmet slapped her with the back of her hand and Eden tumbled backwards. The last thing she saw before her head slammed against the machine was Velma landing on Mrs. Emmet's head and she dove for the gun.

Eden felt the warm blood running down the back of her neck. She lay on her side on a hard surface, handcuff still on her wrist. She knew the warm body snuggled behind her was Lucas from the smell of spearmint. A rough tongue scratched her nose so she turned her head and dried the ickiness on her shoulder. She tried to open her eyes but her pounding head refused. She had to know where—or when—they were.

Loud pounding above her reverberated throughout the small confines.

Eden forced her eyes open. Two dark brown eyes less only inches away met hers. Velma purred happily and rubbed her head against Eden's cheek. With one hand handcuffed to Lucas and the other trapped under her body, Eden was at the mercy of Velma's affection.

Her body bounced as Lucas again and again pounded his large fist into the glass tube encasing them. "Let us out of here!"

Eden winced from the pain shooting through her ears and head. She was in the time machine with Lucas, but nothing had happened yet.

Her eyes adjusted just in time to make eye contact with Mrs. Emmet as she pressed a button on the keyboard.

Suddenly, the world disappeared in a blinding flash of light.

Chapter 31

The sudden darkness hurt Eden's eyes. Nausea followed the sensation that she had blacked out, again. And why did it feel as if the room was spinning out of control?

"That was weird as hell!"

Lucas was still behind her.

Darkness turned bright. A sound like decompression echoed as the glass door on the end of the tube opened, and two guys in dark suits held guns aimed at the trapped duo. She didn't care; they were still in the lab in Halstead and she took that as a good sign. "I can't say when we are, but I don't think we're in Russia." She quickly prayed it wasn't thirty years later.

The two gunmen ignored Velma, who, for the first time, couldn't wait to get away from Eden and Lucas. She bound past them and out the door.

The time traveling duo slowly crawled out of the machine, Eden holding the back of her bleeding head.

"We just traveled in time!" Lucas sounded as excited as Eden would expect him to after winning the state tournament.

"Oh, so *now* you believe!"

"I never doubted you." His mischievous grin was almost comforting.

"Apology accepted."

"What now?" Lucas asked.

A brightness drew Eden's attention to a petite lady holding a video camera that shined a light directly on them. One of the two dark-suited men made a call on his cell phone. "Sir, we have a situation here. It's the two kids."

Once the FBI agents confirmed that Eden and Lucas were the two teenagers who had gone missing, they removed the handcuffs and bandaged Eden's head.

Mickey arrived in jeans, a t-shirt, and a bed head for the ages—a stark contrast to his regular clean-cut uniform look. Eden relaxed because Mickey didn't look like he had aged. He threw his arms around his cousin, putting Lucas clearly out of his comfort zone. How long had they been away?

"Eden!"

She got her own hug from Maimeo.

Eden and Lucas sat in chairs in the same lobby they had snuck through days earlier to get their first glance of the machine. This time, instead of being empty, two long tables held pizza boxes, chips, and soda. A woman in a dark pants suit entered the lobby, filled a plate with pizza and chips, then left with the plate and a cup of coffee.

Maimeo, who a few minutes earlier had chased off the FBI lady recording them, helped herself and brought pizza to the two teenagers. Mickey filled two Solo cups with ice from an ice chest on the floor, then set them in front of Eden and Lucas along with a half empty two-liter bottle of Dr. Pepper. He must have noticed Eden observing the FBI agent.

"There are several agents stationed around the outside of the hospital, to make sure no one gets to the machine."

Lucas poured himself a cup of Dr. Pepper, then filled Eden's cup. He removed a pepperoni and held it down for Velma, who took it and settled under his chair. "Are they that worried someone will try to steal it?"

"Can you imagine the ramifications of a time machine?" Eden contemplated. "It can be a dangerous tool."

Maimeo shook her head. "Imagine that…a real time machine right here in Halstead."

"It was Mrs. Emmet," Lucas told Mickey. "She knew we knew about the time machine—" Eden loudly cleared her throat.

"Okay, okay! Eden was the only one who believed it was a time machine and Mrs. Emmet wanted to sell it to the Russians. She had to get rid of us in order to keep Eden quiet."

Mickey sighed. "We know. We have Mrs. Emmet in custody, but she won't talk. She was deep in debt from her gambling losses. The feds think she found out about the time machine and killed Mayor Washburn in order to collect on the money from the sale to the Russians."

"She put us in the time machine to send us three months into the future. How did we come back so soon?" Eden asked.

Lucas blushed. "When Mrs. Emmet knelt down to check on you after she knocked you out I changed the travel time from three months to three hours."

"Really?" After she said it, she felt bad for her surprised reaction. "I'm sorry I hit you so hard. I wasn't mad."

He shrugged. "It's okay, it wasn't that hard."

"How did you change our travel time with only one hand and without Mrs. Emmet knowing it?"

"It only took a mouse click to change months to hours. I guess I was quick, and luckily she didn't notice."

"A few hours?" Mickey shook his head vigorously. You've been missing for three days.

"What?" Eden and Lucas shouted in unison.

"We were gone for three days?"

Mickey retrieved his phone from his pocket. "It's one eighteen, Sunday night... well, Monday morning."

"That's not how I expected my first weekend away with a girl to go."

Mickey and Eden stared at Lucas blankly.

Maimeo glared.

"What? That was funny, you have to admit."

Mickey ignored the comment. "The night you disappeared, Ashley brought us the book she'd copied for you; Mayor Washburn's journal detailing the time machine."

Lucas exclaimed, "What? How did you copy his journal?"

"After I retrieved the book from Mrs. Emmet's house, I ran by The Pizza Parlor and asked Ashley to copy it for me. I couldn't let the information get away."

"While I was being held at gunpoint?"

She gave him a pleading look. "It's a super speedy copier."

Mickey continued. "Officer Dirks notified the FBI immediately. It took a lot of convincing just to get them to send one agent up from Wichita; thought it was a big joke. Once that agent took a look at the evidence, though, we had a whole slew of them in town. They set up a trap and caught Mrs. Emmet, Boris Yugov and two other Russian operatives inspecting the machine and making plans to transport it. That was in the middle of the night Saturday night. Of course, as you see, it's well guarded now.

"Anyhow, at first Mrs. Emmet didn't say anything. Finally she confessed to putting you two into the time machine."

"And Velma," Lucas interrupted.

"Who's Velma?" Mickey asked.

Lucas picked up the gray kitten and fed her another pepperoni. "Meet Velma, the first kitten time traveler."

Mickey looked unimpressed and Eden was anxious to hear more. "You said Mrs. Emmet confessed to forcing us into the time machine?"

Mickey nodded. "I think she felt awful about it. But she refuses to say anything else. Said the only person she would talk to is you."

Eden's eyebrows rose. "Me? Why me?"

"She won't say. Maybe she's stalling, or maybe she really wants to talk to you."

"Do you think she is responsible for Mayor Washburn's death?" Eden asked hesitantly.

Mickey sighed, seemingly unsure of what to say. "It's possible. But the evidence points elsewhere."

Mickey had stopped making eye contact, making Eden nervous. "Jessica?"

He nodded. "We have her in custody. Yesterday morning we received an envelope in the mail with recordings of Jessica and Mayor Washburn discussing the time machine.

"Dr. Emmet wanted to turn the machine over to the government, but Mayor Washburn and Jessica wanted to sell it. We think they were trying to sell it without the doctor knowing.

"On the recordings, the mayor and Jessica had some heated arguments about who to sell the time machine to and for what price. The D.A. thinks there is enough money involved and enough evidence for him to get a first-degree murder conviction.

"That's not all you missed. This afternoon all the media outlets in the area and the major news organizations in the country received certified letters from Dr. Roger Emmet."

Eden and Lucas gasped. "So he's okay?"

"He claims he's traveling in time and will reappear at noon on Monday, today. We've been flooded with calls."

Eden beamed. "Just like I said!"

"It looks like it," Mickey acknowledged.

"Do you think Jessica killed Mayor Gaylord?" Eden asked.

"The evidence is overwhelming," Mickey said.

"I don't know…" she started.

"There is the twenty-dollar bill you showed Officer Dirks that said 'she knows.' It sounded like he was concerned about Jessica. He included a note with the recordings that one of the reasons he used the time machine was to hide from Jessica and Mayor Washburn. They were arguing and he thought Jessica was dangerous. He tried to talk the mayor into going with him, but he declined.

"He also wrote that Jessica had a surveillance system. She had secretly kept strict tabs of what he did while in his lab. He felt trapped, stalked. He gave instructions to where Jessica kept the hidden recordings and suggested we check them to verify his story."

"And...?" Eden urged.

Mickey looked up. Eden thought his eyes were moist. "We found her surveillance system. Her room had been trashed. We found the recordings like the doctor said, but the time he claimed he left in the machine and the evening of the murder of Mayor Washburn had been erased."

Eden gasped. That was supposed to have been the proof!

Mickey struggled to continue, and then he shot a pained glance at Lucas. "Your fingerprints are all over her system."

"Of course they are!" Lucas said excitedly. "We found her system and recordings. We were going to notify you after we met with Mrs. Emmet."

"I'm sorry," Mickey choked out. "Officer Dirks believes that you erased the recordings. The evidence suggests you were her accomplice."

"But he didn't do it!" Eden protested. "I was with him the whole time."

"Yes, we know. Your prints were also found all over the room. I'm afraid you're both under arrest. You have the right to remain silent..."

Chapter 32

E den and Lucas spent the next hour in an interrogation room, the same room in which Officer Dirks had chewed them out days earlier. Maimeo had come and gone; promised to find a good lawyer.

With nothing to lose, Eden had agreed to speak with Mrs. Emmet, on the condition she try to get Mrs. Emmet to confess.

As she approached the other interrogation room, she hesitated before opening the door. Her anger had turned to sorrow and she debated whether she could go through with it. She quickly opened the door before she changed her mind.

Mrs. Emmet gasped, and for a minute Eden thought she might faint. Slowly she rose from her seat behind the table, wrists handcuffed together. She stared at Eden as if she were a ghost.

"What?" Eden demanded a lot more forcefully than she meant.

Mrs. Emmet stood with her mouth open, silent for several long moments. A tear ran down her left cheek and her bottom lip began to quiver.

Eden wasn't buying it. All the goodwill Mrs. Emmet had built with Eden had been shattered in the lab three days ago when she'd kidnapped Lucas and sent them both through the time machine, willing to trade their lives, and her husband's, for money. She continued to glare, steeled against the emotional basket case on the other side of the table.

"I-I-I don't believe it." Mrs. Emmet swung her arm blindly behind her in search of the chair. Finally her hand made contact and she slowly sat, eyes glued to Eden. "I'm so glad you're okay."

"Oh, stop that hogwash! You kidnapped Lucas, blackmailed me, and then sent us both to what easily could have been our deaths." Eden hadn't planned to explode, and wondered if she shouldn't let herself out before she physically attacked the woman.

"I'm truly sorry. I lost myself."

"Maybe you found your true self."

She dropped her head in shame, the first sign that maybe she *was* sorry.

Eden turned the chair around and sat with her arms across the backrest. "Lucas changed the time so we only traveled for three days instead of three months."

"I know you don't believe me, and I can't say that I blame you, but I am glad you're safe. I have been in debt for so long, and with the opportunity to put my hands on billions of dollars… well, it was too much to pass up. I am sorry, but I have to be honest. If I had the chance again I'm sure I would make the same decision, as much as I would like to say I would do the right thing."

Eden scowled. "I can understand your willingness to risk Lucas and me for the money, but your husband?"

"Oh, I know. I love Roger, I truly do. But we haven't been close for years. He's always put his work above me—above everything. That's why we never had kids. He didn't want parenthood to distract him from his career. I was foolish and vain enough to accept his decision but as the years went by and as I became lonelier, I turned to gambling. I lost control and racked up an exorbitant debt. I couldn't resist the temptation of selling the time machine for two billion dollars, even if it meant losing Roger."

Sadness replaced anger in Eden's heart. This lady was lonely. So lonely she would commit these crimes and risk the lives of others. Eden understood, and vowed to do what she could to avoid that level of loneliness, even though that was all she had ever known.

"What happened? When did you learn about the time machine?"

"I didn't know anything about it until you told me that's what you thought happened to Roger. After our visit, I started putting the pieces together in my mind and things began to make sense. The time machine would explain why I thought I had slept for nine days that one time.

"That's when I decided to steal Gaylord's diary from Jessica and see what more I could learn. I had to know what Roger had been up to all these years. When I read about the upcoming sale of the machine to the Russians and Roger's desire to give it to science instead of selling it, well, that sounded just like him. He would rather have had the prestige and recognition than a billion dollars, or two.

"I figured since Roger and Gaylord were both out of the picture, well, I see how foolish it was now, but I couldn't resist the opportunity to go after that much money."

"You do realize you may spend the rest of your life in prison? Was it worth it?"

"At least I won't have to worry about my debt if I'm in jail." she said without conviction. Eden thought Mrs. Emmet was trying to convince herself that jail was a desired option. Desired or not, she would have to learn to live with it—how could she get out of kidnapping charges? Or threatening to kill Lucas? Eden didn't know how the legal issues would play out. But what a sad state that she could find relief from time in jail.

Mrs. Emmet sounded sincere. Now it was time to ask the question Eden needed the answer to most.

"Mrs. Emmet, did you kill Mayor Washburn?"

Chapter 33

*E*den rested her head on her arms and tried not to cry. Her exhaustion allowed her well-kept emotions to rule. Oh, for a bed. She couldn't have slept more than a few minutes when the door burst open.

"The Royals were down by five runs in the bottom of the ninth inning and came back to win." Mickey carried an eight by eleven manila folder and tossed it on the table.

"I can't believe I missed the comeback," Lucas complained. "I was… I was… If I was traveling in time while it happened, does that mean I didn't exist yesterday afternoon? Or was I a bunch of mixed-up particles and atoms floating in space?"

"Maybe you were in another dimension," Mickey offered. "Oh hey, maybe we can go back in time and go to the game."

"Eden said we can't go back in time, just forward. Isn't that right, Eden?"

Hearing her name helped her pass through the fog. "Um, yeah. At least that's the theory."

Mickey pulled out his phone and handed it to Lucas. Eden peered over his shoulder. The picture was from Dr. Emmet's lab; a dark-haired woman wearing a beige pant suit peered at the time machine. Her mouth was awkwardly open, probably caught in the midst of talking. Eden guessed her hair would flow down most of her back when let loose from the bun. Although young—probably Mickey's age—her eyes said she was all business.

"That's Cereena."

Lucas whistled. "She *is* a looker. And she gave you her number?"

"Well, no. I gave her my card and she said she might call after the case is wrapped up."

Eden chuckled. She didn't mean for it to be audible.

"What? You don't think Mickey's good enough for her?"

"Why would you assume she was thinking bad things about me? She probably thinks you're weird for thinking she's attractive."

"She laughed because she doesn't think Cereena's interested in you."

"I'm sorry." Eden said, too tired for the bickering. "I don't think she'll ever call. If she was truly interested, she would have given you her number."

Lucas argued. "A lot of girls won't give out their numbers anymore. It's a safety thing."

"That's true. But Mickey and Cereena are both law enforcement. There's little risk in providing her number if she was interested."

Mickey sighed sadly and changed the subject. "Did Mrs. Emmet tell you anything useful?"

"She apologized. I really don't think she knew anything about the time machine before she read Mayor Washburn's journal after stealing it from Jessica. I'm convinced she had nothing to do with her husband's disappearance or Mayor Washburn's death."

Officer Johnson dumped dozens of pictures from the unmarked manila envelope. Eden absentmindedly sifted through the pictures before her. Most were shots of the time machine, like the photographer tried to get a picture of every nook and cranny. There were pictures of the murder scene and Eden quickly tossed the pictures of Mayor Washburn's dead body aside. She had no stomach for it.

"Wait, are these pictures evidence?"

"Not exactly," Mickey said, hesitantly. "I had copies made."

Lucas picked up a few pictures and thumbed through them. "Why make copies?"

"Because we're not allowed to handle evidence. We're suspects." She viewed a few more photos. "This isn't exactly by the book, Officer Johnson."

"I'm desperate." Mickey, too, flipped through the pictures. "I know you two weren't involved with Mayor

Washburn's murder, so I'm looking for anything that can clear you."

The images began to blur. Eden buried her head in her arms, tired and frustrated. Morning would arrive any time, Mrs. Emmet was locked up, Dr. Emmet would return in a few hours, and Eden gave up.

"Eden, we have to figure this out."

"Don't you get it? There's nothing more we can do. The police and the FBI are in control. Maybe they'll eventually figure out the truth, but I doubt it. They got an answer and that will be good enough. Welcome to the system. Come visit me, if you're lucky enough to negotiate probation. I won't be so lucky this time."

Lucas sat, dejected. Eden looked away, sad to burst his little hopeful bubble, but he might as well face the truth now.

Mickey continued to desperately sort through pictures, but Lucas had settled on one photo to hold.

"I wonder if they'll let me keep this picture." He set the picture in front of him.

Eden picked up the photo of Lucas and her, with her pointing at the time machine. She remembered the moment, her best since coming to Halstead. With her intense face and mouth slightly open, the picture was taken while she explained her theory of how the doctor had gone back in time. Between her and Lucas sat the blank screened monitor that controlled the time machine. Lucas towered over the monitor, focused on her giving her explanation. It was a good profile picture of him. He wasn't bad-looking. Okay, who was she kidding? He was gorgeous, and although he was still obnoxious, he was starting to grow on her. She smiled—couldn't help it.

"It's a good picture of you," she told him, "but do you really need another picture of yourself?"

"I don't want it because *I'm* in it."

Eden felt her face burn. "I look silly."

"That's so you! You're intense, like a bulldog, solving the case. This shows your fire. You really did an amazing job to figure out Dr. Emmet had invented a time machine."

She was too embarrassed to look at Lucas, so she stared at the time machine. It was surreal. A time machine had been invented and really worked. And she had even gotten a free ride.

Suddenly her eyes went wide. "The monitor is blank!"

"What?"

"The monitor is blank!" she hollered again.

"So?" Lucas and Mickey asked.

"I know who killed Mayor Washburn!"

Chapter 34

*E*den leaned her head against the back door of the police car. She clutched a copy of Mayor Washburn's journal close to her chest, wishing it was a pillow and the car seat her bed. Although she had only been in the car for less than five minutes, something about riding in the back of vehicles that made her sleepy. That, and staying awake for four days… technically. She knew Sam would detest seeing her, especially with a police escort. She couldn't help thinking how she had called the police on Sam out at the lake, which had turned out to be a big misunderstanding. This time, though, she had the facts on her side. Sam wouldn't welcome them, but he wouldn't be able to argue once she laid out the case. She hoped he would cooperate.

Officer Dirks knocked on Sam's door, then pounded. Twice. Finally Sam opened the door a few inches and squinted from the dark inside.

"What do you want?"

Officers Dirks and Johnson blocked Eden's view. "May we come in? We need to talk."

"What about?"

"It's about the murder of Mayor Washburn," Officer Dirks said.

"I already told you all I know. At the station. Remember? When you arrested me and took me to jail, then let me go? *I* remember."

"I think I can straighten this out quickly." Eden peered around Officer Dirks and Sam scowled. He obviously hadn't realized she was present.

He glared at her with hate-filled eyes. "I've had enough of you. How dare you bring her to my house after the trouble she's caused me?"

Eden quickly jumped in. "I know who killed Mayor Washburn, and I know it wasn't you."

Now it was Officer Dirks' turn to be agitated. "I thought you were revealing the murderer for us. Why bring us here if Sam didn't kill the mayor?"

Eden answered the question by speaking to Sam. "I know what really happened to your son, and if you give me a chance to explain, I can help give you some closure on your Shaggy's death."

Sam was quiet for several moments, probably pondering whether to trust Eden's excuse for waking him from his hangover-induced sleep. He was understandably suspicious. "Assuming you know something I don't, why would you tell me?"

"First, I'm awfully sorry for the trouble I've caused. I was wrong to jump to conclusions as I did and accuse you of murdering Mrs. Emmet. I'm sorry. Also, I need your help to prove who killed Mayor Washburn."

Apparently Sam couldn't pass up the potential news about his son and the opportunity to help prove the identification of the murderer. He shuffled through the mess that was his floor and collapsed into his chair, leaving the door ajar for the four visitors to make their own way into his home. They all remained standing.

"I know for twenty years you've thought Dr. Emmet's negligence during surgery caused your son's death. I need to tell you that you were only half right."

Sam didn't look at her, not once. He stared straight ahead, in the direction of the blank screen on the forty-four-inch television hanging from the wall. His face remained cold, frozen, except for the tears that slid down his cheeks. He didn't flinch but let them run uncontested the whole time Eden spoke.

"I've copied some passages from Mayor Washburn's journal. It tells the truth about what happened to your son. I'll leave them to read when you want, but to summarize, you were right that your son died due to surgical negligence, but it wasn't by Dr. Emmet, it was by the mayor."

"What?" It was Lucas, the only one in the room other than Sam who hadn't read the account for himself.

"It's all in the mayor's own handwriting. The truth haunted him, because he allowed his friend, Dr. Emmet, to take the blame and the professional risk when you sued him.

"As you know, it was partly the mayor's testimony on Dr. Emmet's behalf that helped sway the verdict for the doctor.

"In reality, Dr. Washburn was saving his own skin.

"Dr. Emmet hadn't been feeling well that day, so at the last minute Dr. Washburn joined him in the surgery. It was Dr. Washburn whose reactions and decision-making weren't fast enough to save your son. He had been in administration for a couple of years and was out of practice and it cost your son's life. I'm sorry. It's all right here in the mayor's own words."

After several long moments of quiet, Sam tried to speak, but he couldn't compose himself.

"I know you need some time alone to process this. I hate to ask you for a favor, but I need your help to prove who murdered Mayor Washburn. I need to borrow your journal."

"Why do you need his journal?" Mickey asked.

"Sam documented a lot of things that went on at the hospital. In particular, he saw a ghost in Dr. Emmet's lab about the night Mayor Washburn was killed."

"I knew there were ghosts!" Lucas exclaimed, much too excitedly for the somber atmosphere.

"Where are you going with this?" Officer Dirks asked.

"It will all be clear once we get to the lab," Eden assured him.

Sam continued to stare ahead, lost in his own emotions. He reached between the cushions of his chair, then stretched out his arm, offering his journal.

Eden took the journal. Sam firmly grabbed her by the wrist and broke his eye contact with the blank TV to look her in the eyes. How he could see through the tears she didn't know. He struggled with all his might and finally said, "Thank you."

He released his grip and returned to his own world. Eden hoped he would be okay.

She turned to Officer Dirks, ready to move on. "We'll need Jessica to meet us at the doctor's lab."

Chapter 35

*A*t least a hundred media vans filled the hospital parking lot. Eden recognized the Wichita television station's call letters, a few of the radio stations, and some national networks as well.

Eden, Lucas, and Jessica alighted from the police car with Officers Dirks and Johnson. A hush spread across the parking lot. The cameras all turned on them and for a brief moment it was eerily quiet, until the first reporter darted their way, shouting, "Officer, what can you tell us about the reports of a time machine inside the hospital?"

Officer Dirks determinedly strode through the gathering sea of reporters as the rest of the group did their best to stay in his wake. Three soldiers dressed in camouflage uniforms stood guard at the front entrance.

"It looks like they're guarding Fort Knox," Lucas commented.

"This place is surrounded by military," Mickey whispered back to Lucas.

One of the soldiers got on his phone to confirm the group's credentials before allowing them inside.

Another four soldiers relaxed in the lobby along with several men in dark suits, all enjoying pizza from The Pizza Parlor.

Dr. Emmet's lab still contained two FBI agents—different ones than had greeted Eden and Lucas a few hours earlier—and a documenter, the same lady in wire-rimmed glasses and a pant suit that filmed Eden and Lucas's return from the machine.

The clock on the wall said 11:44.

Officer Dirks got right to business. "Eden, why don't you tell us who you suspect killed Mayor Washburn?"

"First of all I will start by telling you who didn't. Lucas didn't do it because I was with him that evening when he was in here."

Officer Dirks raised his eyebrow.

"And afterwards."

"How do we know you didn't conspire together?" Officer Dirks pressed.

"A fair question, and one I believe will clear itself up once I identify the real killer. For now, let's leave it at that—I know Lucas didn't do it because I was with him."

"Proceed," Officer Dirks granted.

Eden continued. "Mrs. Emmet has a gambling problem and her habit has gotten her and the doctor deep in debt. That's why she stole Mayor Washburn's journal from Jessica's house. When I told her about my theory of the time machine and the book I had seen Jessica sneak out of the hospital, Mrs. Emmet put some details together. She had once slept for nine days, or so she'd thought.

"What really happened was one night after taking her sleeping medicine and turning in for the night, Dr. Emmet and Mayor Washburn carried her to the hospital and put her in the time machine. They had thoroughly tested the machine for short periods of time, including on themselves, and on animals over long periods of time. They needed a person to travel in time for several days.

"But they were concerned about being gone that long and drawing unnecessary attention to themselves, so they decided Mrs. Emmet would make a great test subject. She wouldn't be missed by others like they would. They put her in the machine and sent her nine days ahead.

"Even though nine days had passed, her body only slept for one night. They made up the story that she had been asleep that long and she naturally believed them. But after she knew about the time machine it all made sense. She confirmed that in the mayor's journal.

"She also learned in his journal that there had been an agreement made between Mayor Washburn and the Russians to sell the time machine for two billion dollars. That was too much money for Mrs. Emmet to pass up. She contacted the Russians to try to complete the sale. She figured since Mayor Washburn and her husband were both out of the picture that she could pull it off, disappear, and enjoy the money, which would be enough to satisfy her gambling addiction for the rest of her life.

"She did not, however, have anything to do with the doctor's disappearance or the mayor's death. She simply tried to take advantage of the situation that presented itself so nicely for her."

"How can you be certain she didn't have anything to do with the doctor or the mayor?" Officer Johnson asked.

"She told me," Eden stated flatly.

"She could be lying," Jessica said.

"I don't think so. Besides, she wasn't alone that evening."

"What?" several of them asked.

"Sam was in the neighborhood, as we have previously established, raising a ruckus. He had drunk a little more than usual that night and passed out in Mrs. Emmet's yard. In spite of her shortcomings, she has a big heart and tried to wake him to go home. He tried to get up but could hardly walk. He stumbled to her porch and passed out again. In the night chill, Mrs. Emmet worried about his health and covered him with her quilt.

"Sometime during the night or early the next morning, Sam woke and went home, taking the quilt with him. Still inebriated, he crashed for a while longer. When he woke, he didn't know where the quilt had come from. When his cat, Mrs. Thomas, passed away, he wrapped her in the quilt and that's what Lucas and I saw—Sam taking his cat to the lake to bury her."

"And when Sam left Mrs. Emmet's porch that night he left his lighter behind," Mickey added.

"Yes. Mrs. Emmet found it the next day. She brought it inside and set it in her parlor, where we found it after the Russians had trashed her home looking for evidence of where Dr. Emmet might be or information about the time machine."

"So if it wasn't Sam or Stephanie, then we were right. It was Jessica," Officer Dirks said.

"No, Jessica truly loved Mayor Washburn. They planned to buy an island with the money from the time machine and move away together."

"But we found the murder weapon in her office!" Mickey said. "She was the only other one at the hospital during that time except for you and Lucas.

"I believe she was framed by the real murderer."

"By whom?" Officer Dirks asked skeptically. "Who else could have done it?"

Eden pointed to the monitor. "The answer was revealed to me by this monitor."

"But it's blank," Mickey said.

"Exactly!" Eden cheered. "After some time of not being used, the monitor goes to sleep." She pressed the enter key and some words and numbers slowly came into view on the screen. "When Lucas and I first entered this room the night of the murder, the screen looked similar to what we see now. It would have been blank, unless someone had recently used it."

"You're saying that someone used the time machine before you arrived?" Officer Dirks asked.

"I believe that when Dr. Emmet left in the time machine Saturday evening, he programmed it so he would return Monday evening."

"Why would he do that?" Mickey asked.

"To kill his partner."

"But Roger and Gaylord were friends," Officer Dirks chimed in.

"They were partners, but they were far apart on the issue of what to do with the time machine. Dr. Emmet wanted the prestige that went with inventing a time machine, but Mayor Washburn wanted to sell it to the highest bidder on the black market. The mayor wanted to sell it for the money. Dr. Emmet wanted the notoriety and fame that would come from inventing a time machine more than he wanted wealth. Even though Dr. Emmet had invented the machine, Mayor Washburn owned his inventions and controlled what was to be done with them.

"As owner of the hospital, Jessica could potentially have legal rights to the time machine since it was located in her facility.

"Mayor Washburn and Dr. Emmet had agreed to keep the secret from Jessica, but the mayor told her about it and Dr. Emmet found out. He needed to get her out of the way as well as Mayor Washburn in order to achieve his goal. With the sale approaching, Dr.

Emmet was desperate, so he came up with a scheme to get credit for his invention.

"He returned Monday evening around nine. He knew that Mayor Washburn and Jessica regularly got together after the city council meetings to talk hospital business. Then the mayor's routine brought him up here to the lab to check on Dr. Emmet and the time machine. When Mayor Washburn entered the room that evening, Dr. Emmet stuck him with the syringe.

"What he hadn't planned on was Lucas and I showing up. He had probably tapped into Jessica's video surveillance system and saw us coming. He couldn't afford for the mayor's body to be discovered yet because Jessica would have video of him murdering the mayor and he needed time to erase it. Dr. Emmet did what he had to do—he took Mayor Washburn into the time machine with him. That's why the screen was not blank when we came in. Dr. Emmet needed to hide until we left, so he went ahead in time a few hours. Then he returned, and left the mayor's body in the adjacent room.

"He wasn't done, though. After he had the mayor's body in place, he snuck down to Jessica's office and planted the syringe. Then he erased the video evidence. This kept the police from seeing it was him but also made them suspicious because it looked like Jessica had erased the evidence. Before he had left in the time machine the first time, he had arranged for the delivery of the notices to the news organizations."

"And you're saying because he revealed when he was going to return that that would create interest and give him media coverage?" Mickey asked.

"With the mayor dead and Jessica framed for the murder, the time machine would be his alone to do with what he wanted," Lucas added.

"It's a great theory, but can you prove any of it?" Officer Dirks asked.

"That's why I had you bring Sam's journal," Eden said. "He kept a close watch on Dr. Emmet and Mayor Washburn. There should be sufficient evidence in there about their disagreements on how to use the time machine. The night Mayor Washburn was killed, Sam told Mrs. Emmet he saw Dr. Emmet's ghost. She told me about it when I asked her if she had killed the mayor. Sam hadn't seen a ghost, like he thought. He had actually seen Dr. Emmet up in his lab.

"You saw Lucas's pictures when you confiscated his phone, so you know he has a picture of a coffee mug on that desk (she pointed) from the night of the murder. If Dr. Emmet arrives with the mug that will prove he was here that night. But also, I would think the FBI could do a diagnostic of the time machine and obtain the history of its use, which would show that the machine was used several times the night of the murder. And I bet with a little investigative work you should be able to trace the package the doctor sent to the police to where it came from and when it was sent."

Suddenly the time machine began to sputter and within a few moments Dr. Emmet lay inside the glass tube, with the coffee cup Eden and Lucas had seen the night of the murder. The documenter continued to snap pictures. Mickey helped Dr. Emmet out and immediately placed him in handcuffs. "You have the right to remain silent…"

Chapter 36

The next day Eden sat inside on her grandma's back porch reading when a loud knock on the back door caused her to startle. Lucas quickly opened and shut the door behind him.

"Have you looked out your front door? It's crazy out there!"

"Yeah, I was scheduled to work but Toby called and asked me not to come in. They've had reporters stop by all morning asking about me."

"On the positive side, we had great media coverage for our baseball practice this morning. My parents made Mickey give me a ride to and from practice in the police car."

"It sucks—we do something good and now we can't leave the house. It seems all backwards."

Lucas plopped down on the loveseat. "You know what else is all backwards? Dr. Emmet. Sure, he got arrested for murder, but he got everything he wanted. Look at all the publicity he's receiving. There are reporters from all over the world. I'll bet he even gets a great book deal when this all over."

"Has Mickey said what's going to happen with the time machine?" Eden asked.

"The FBI will move it to a secret government facility later this week. It's all hush-hush."

"Maybe they'll take the reporters with them," Eden quipped.

"I don't know. Mrs. Emmet stands accused of kidnapping and Dr. Emmet will eventually have a trial for murder, probably in Wichita."

Eden sighed. "I guess these reporters won't be going away anytime soon."

Lucas turned serious. "I'm worried about Velma."

"Oh?"

He crossed his arms and shook his head. "I didn't see her while we were at the hospital yesterday. I tried to look for her today, but with the feds guarding the time machine it's hard to get close to the hospital. Mickey said the agents hadn't been very nice to Velma."

"I'm sure she'll turn up soon."

Lucas sulked, looking unconvinced.

Eden went to the kitchen and returned a moment later, setting a saucer of milk on the floor in front of Lucas.

His look of confusion turned to delight when Velma bounded around the corner to lap from the dish.

Lucas scooped her up. "Velma!"

The truth must have registered with him because his face filled with shock. "How did she get here?"

Eden shrugged, trying to downplay her involvement. "I heard she was being mistreated and didn't want you to try to rescue her so I told Mickey to get her out. He asked Cereena to help him smuggle her out and she was so touched she asked him out."

Lucas set Velma down so she could drink the milk. "So how did you end up with her?"

"I guess Mickey misunderstood me telling him to get her out as me wanting to take care of her." In truth, she had asked Mickey to bring her the kitten and then persuaded Maimeo to keep it, but she would deny it.

"So, why you?"

The question caught Eden off guard. "Why me, what?"

"Why did the old doctor give you the twenty-dollar bill?"

"I think it was just chance. I was new in town and he assumed his strange behavior and the scribbling on the bill would cause me to give it to the police after he disappeared. It was part of his plan to frame Jessica and he needed it to get to the police while seeming like he was scared."

Lucas nodded, though didn't look convinced.

"Or maybe we'll have to read his book to find out the truth."

They sat for a couple of awkward moments before Eden asked. "Do you want to stay for lunch? I think I'll make spaghetti."

"Sure," Lucas said with a wry grin. "But first, let me take off my shoes."

Support the Author

Thank you for reading *When the Time is Right*. I appreciate the time you invested in my story and trust that since you made it this far, you enjoyed the ride. As an independent author, I don't have a large publishing company promoting my books. I could use your help. Please consider doing at least one of the following.

Review
Leave a review on the online location where you purchased the book or on my website. Reviews are a critical tool for getting my books noticed.

Buy another book
Look at the other books I've written and published. Maybe there's another one you might like.

Share
Tell your friends and family what you liked about reading *When the Time is Right*. If they show interest, encourage them to read it.

Connect
Sign up for Bill's mailing list and get regular updates on future writing projects:
   www.billbushauthor.com/sign-up-for-e-mail-list/
Visit Bill's webpage for more information about his writings:
   www.billbushauthor.com
Connect directly with the author by sending an email:
   bill@billbushauthor.com

The Next Book in the Series

Halstead Mysteries 2: Three Blind Mice

ISBN 978-1-945871-16-0

turn the page for a sample

You haven't had enough? Watch out for Eden's next adventure, for one thing is certain. Once a sleuth, always a sleuth. And that cat won't let her rest either. Sign up for my publishing alerts to stay informed about new releases in this series:

www.billbushauthor.com/sign-up-for-e-mail-list/

Chapter 1

Shit! Why did he agree to meet this late? After umpiring four games, Derek's body screamed for the queen sized bed in his perfectly cooled sixty-two degree hotel room.

Instead, sweat beaded on his forehead from the humid night air. Just great. Now he would need another shower before bed.

His stomach churned and he rubbed it soothingly. He was still stuffed from an above average hotel buffet—at the expense of the Kansas State High School Athletic Association, of course. Hopefully the meeting would be quick; he had a sudden urge that would soon require toilet paper.

He had nearly fallen asleep during Sportscenter when he received a call, saying they had information regarding a conspiracy to throw the tournament. This was high school baseball, for Christ's sake. What could be the benefit of throwing it?

Wouldn't talk over the phone, of course. Yapped on and on, all paranoid; thought the phones were bugged. If he hadn't known them for so long he would have blown the rant off as madness. But this was one of the sanest persons he knew. So he threw on jeans and a t-shirt, grabbed a stogy and casually wandered to the edge of the tree line, the designated meeting spot.

The sprinklers watered the outfields on the, what, a dozen or so ball fields. A softball tournament occupied four of them this weekend. Derek thought about thirty teams were involved.

The tournament he was umpiring—the High School 3A State Baseball Championship tournament—only required one field. Eight teams. Single elimination. They should have played it out in two days, but they stretched it to three. He had no idea why. Extra day of per diem for him, though.

A quiet and serene complex for all the activity it had seen that day. The only activity lay on the basketball court as several sweaty teenagers played full court. It was nearly midnight.

His cigar was nearly half gone before he heard footsteps. But they came from the woods, not from the hotels.

He stepped back and gaped at his visitor. It wasn't his appointment, but that didn't seem to matter.

"Hi Derek. What are you doing here?"

He hadn't prepared a lie; hadn't expected to see anyone he knew at this time of night.

He lifted the cigar and smiled. "Enjoying a relaxing pleasure before bed. What are you doing about?"

"Same."

What was the guilty pleasure? Running? Sweat dropped from the chin, t-shirt spotted, and the breathing was short and quick. Derek puffed and nodded at the aluminum his friend carried.

"Batting practice?"

"I wouldn't think of hiking without protection. You never know what kind of trouble one might come upon." The mischievous smile sent shivers throughout Derek's body. Had it turned cooler?

Derek's caller wouldn't likely show while he had company. It didn't matter except they would likely call and wake him later if Derek didn't meet them now. Maybe if he started walking he could shake his visitor.

"I'm glad you survived your romp in the woods." Derek started away from the tree line. "I'll see you at the game tomorrow."

Just as he thought he would be left alone, the sound of feet shuffled up next to him.

"What do you think of the tournament?"

What kind of question is that? He appeased. "I'd say Scott City looks like the most well-rounded team. If the Walls kid is able to pitch for Halstead, they'll be hard to beat. Those are the favorites as I see it. I know Elkhart has the best record and the #1 seed, but their schedule's been soft and I'm not sure they can handle Scott City tomorrow. Without Walls pitching tomorrow, I'd say it's a toss up between Halstead and Independence."

"That isn't what I meant."

The response to his analysis was anger? What was going on here and why the obsession with him and the tournament? He stopped, now on the edge of one of the three outdoor basketball courts. The court that had been full of players when he first stepped outside his hotel now sat alone, dark, and empty.

"I want to know what you think of the organization of the tournament. Namely, do you think there's any illegal activity taking place?"

What with all of the conspiracies? And why had he been thrust into the middle of it?

"Look, I don't know what you think is going on, and I don't really care. I'm just here to make a few calls, collect a paycheck and get home to my wife. I'm afraid if you're looking for information, you're sniffing up the wrong tree." He turned and puffed his cigar, hoping his words had ended their conversation. They hadn't.

"I'm not looking for information. I'm looking for justice."

He recognized the swoosh sound but didn't have time to react before the aluminum bat connected with the back of his head.

ISBN 978-1-945871-16-0

Maimeo's Puzzle Thoughts

Grandma taught me two important lessons: How to stay connected to loved ones who died and how not to be a lonely old lady. Her love for jigsaw puzzles taught me both.

When I was young, every December my grandparents flew from Washington (the state) to Kansas to spend Christmas break with me, my brother, and my parents. And every year the gift I looked forward to the most was a jigsaw puzzle.

I loved receiving the puzzles because it meant alone time with Grandma. Sometimes the rest of my family would help for a few minutes, but most of the time it was me and Grandma and a million puzzle pieces. At least it seemed like a million pieces to my younger self.

For hours, Grandma and I would talk, laugh, and occasionally make progress on our project. When I was young we worked the puzzle several times during her visit. As I got older and the puzzles got harder, it usually took us most of the break to do both my brother's and mine. My brother wasn't a big fan of the puzzles, but liked to help with the border. Then he'd get bored and run off to do something more active. He didn't mind that Grandma and I finished his puzzle.

We drove to Washington each summer to stay with my grandparents and visit their other daughter, my Aunt Charlene. We spent most of our summer visits outside, but when we had down time I sat with Grandma at her card table and worked on whatever puzzle she had out at the time. But those were hard puzzles and I usually wasn't much help.

Grandma had a sewing room where she hung up several of her puzzles. My favorite was a picture of an old castle, like they have back in Europe during the days of kings and knights. She told me she glued the puzzles and I was a teenager before I realized she didn't mean that she glued the puzzle to the wall.

My grandpa died when I was eleven and Grandma changed. My aunt Charlene said that my grandma spent most of the winter working on puzzles. It must have been true because when we visited that summer she had several hanging on the wall in my Grandpa's old office.

The next summer the guest bedroom walls were covered with puzzles. And I mean covered. There wasn't a blank space on any of the walls in the room.

For several years Grandma spent her time putting puzzles together; until most of the walls in her house were covered.

After my freshman year in high school I got a job at a daycare and couldn't make the summer trips. Instead, Grandma started visiting us in the summer, sometimes for several weeks.

Just like her winter trips, Grandma brought a puzzle for us to work on together. These puzzles were harder and took us weeks to complete. Then Grandma always glued the puzzle, carefully packed it and then mailed it back to Washington to hang on her wall.

After Grandma passed away a few years later we flew back to Washington for her funeral and to help Aunt Charlene clean out Grandma's house. I couldn't believe it, but every wall held two or three layers of puzzles. She had hung hundreds of puzzles in her house.

Aunt Charlene explained that after Grandpa passed away, Grandma spent all of her free time working puzzles. She rarely watched television or movies. Instead, she played music and worked puzzles on her card table. Aunt Charlene said that's how Grandma dealt with her loneliness.

I didn't understand until my Charlie died after forty-two years of marriage. I was alone for the first time and didn't know what to do with myself. I moped, slept, watched television, even tried walking, but I couldn't escape the deep depression.

One day while shopping I saw an old puzzle in a thrift store exactly like one I had done with Grandma nearly half a century earlier. As soon as I dumped the pieces on my dining room table I felt like a young girl, and I swear I could feel grandma's presence. For the first time in weeks I felt calm and, well, not sad.

I did nothing else for a week. I finished the puzzle and found it had six pieces missing, but I didn't care because I felt my grandma's presence for the first time since she had passed away. I glued that puzzle, but when I went to hang it I flashed back to my twenty-one-year-old self taking down dozens of puzzles from Grandma's sewing room. I didn't want that to be me so I packed up my puzzle and decided on a move and a life change.

I had isolated myself in the big city, but I wanted a different life in Halstead; one full of friends and laughter and love. I understood my grandma's loneliness like I never had before, and as much as I loved her, I didn't want to turn into what she did after Grandpa died. So I started going to church and volunteering and even started a book club so that I could meet people and make friends.

I almost always have a puzzle on my dining room table or card table, and I work on them alone sometimes. But I feel closest to Grandma when friends come over to visit, drink coffee, and laugh while we occasionally make progress on the puzzle.

For me, jigsaw puzzles are all about relationships. And while I still deeply miss Grandma and Charlie, I have many new friends that help fill the emptiness. I think Grandma would be proud.

Acknowledgments

I n the fall of 2016 I decided I wanted to try to write a murder mystery. It's taken me four years to go from idea to publishing, and during that time I've had a lot of help.

I want to thank Paul Nicholson and fellow author Barbara Lund for their input into the police procedurals involved in my story. They answered a lot of my questions that kept my story as realistic as possible. That being said, if something in the story isn't quite right, it's either because local laws differ from their familiar jurisdictions or I took liberties to enhance the story.

Early on in the process E.J. Clark, with Silver Jay Editing, provided invaluable feedback and critique. Speaking of invaluable feedback, the members of Holly Lisle's Writing Classes forum are quick with encouragement, assistance, guidance, and friendship, and

I wouldn't be the writer I am today without Holly's classes or the community she's created in her forum.

Holly's writing forum is where I met Katharina Kolata who designed the cover and formatted the book for publication. I think this is the ninth book she's helped me with the cover and/or formatting. She's done another amazing job, also on short notice

I want to thank Azzy Reckess, current owner of the Halstead Hospital, for graciously allowing me to host a book launching/signing party inside the hospital entrance. I can see the hospital from my front porch and I walked past it nearly every day while I wrote the rough draft of When the Time is Right. It is so cool to include the hospital in the genesis of the story's public life.

Finally, I want to thank my late mom, Phyllis Roth Lewis. I loved reading *Encyclopedia Brown*, *The Hardy Boys*, and *The Three Investigators* as a kid. I grew up watching *Perry Mason* and *Ellery Queen* reruns as well as reading *Ellery Queen magazine*. Murder mysteries have been one of my favorite genres and I'm sure that came from Mom's love of not only *Perry Mason* and *Ellery Queen*, but *Agatha Christie* and *Murder She Wrote* as well.